*"I guess cowboys are a whole
different breed of man from what
I'm used to...."*

Tenderness made Kirk's eyes glow like warm
coals. "Maybe if you could see what being a
cowboy is all about, you'd understand."

"Maybe," Shannon said, "but I doubt it." Still,
something inside her made her want to believe
whatever he said.

"Come to the ranch and see what I do. Every day.
I'd like you to see my place."

How could she resist? How could she agree?
"Yes." She barely breathed the word. She knew
she was in trouble. Big trouble. But she couldn't
think of a way to back out now. She'd have to
cloak herself in her professional demeanor. After
all, Kirk was only a student, she reminded herself.
But a tiny voice in her head warned her they'd
already become friends, and she already cared for
this strong yet silent type.

Dear Reader,

From classic love stories to romantic comedies to emotional heart tuggers, Silhouette Romance offers six irresistible novels every month by some of your favorite authors—and some sure to become favorites. Just look at the lineup this month:

In *Most Eligible Dad*, book 2 of Karen Rose Smith's wonderful miniseries THE BEST MEN, a confirmed bachelor becomes a FABULOUS FATHER when he discovers he's a daddy.

A single mother and her precious BUNDLE OF JOY teach an unsmiling man how to love again in *The Man Who Would Be Daddy* by bestselling author Marie Ferrarella.

I Do? I Don't? is the very question a bride-to-be asks herself when a sexy rebel from her past arrives just in time to stop her wedding in Christine Scott's delightful novel.

Marriage? A very happily *un*married police officer finally says "I do" in Gayle Kaye's touching tale *Bachelor Cop*.

In *Family of Three* by Julianna Morris, a man and a woman have to share the same house—with separate bedrooms, of course....

Debut author Leanna Wilson knows no woman can resist a *Strong, Silent Cowboy*—and you won't be able to, either!

I'd love to know what you think of the Romance line. Are there any special kinds of stories you'd like to see more of, less of? Your thoughts are very important to me—after all, these books are for you!

Sincerely,

Melissa Senate,
Senior Editor

Please address questions and book requests to:
Silhouette Reader Service
U.S.: 3010 Walden Ave., P.O. Box 1325, Buffalo, NY 14269
Canadian: P.O. Box 609, Fort Erie, Ont. L2A 5X3

STRONG, SILENT COWBOY

Leanna Wilson

Silhouette®
R O M A N C E™
Published by Silhouette Books
America's Publisher of Contemporary Romance

Dedication:
To Laurel Wilson, my sister by birth, my friend by
choice. Thanks for planting the writing seed and helping
nourish it to grow.

Acknowledgment:
A sincere thanks to Lisa Wilson for her expertise
about speech therapy. Sorry if I strayed for the purpose
of the story.

 SILHOUETTE BOOKS

ISBN 0-373-19179-0

STRONG, SILENT COWBOY

Copyright © 1996 by Leanna Ellis

This edition published by arrangement with Harlequin Books S.A.

Printed in U.S.A.

LEANNA WILSON

grew up in Dallas, Texas, and taught elementary school for five years. When the writing bug bit her, she quit teaching to write full-time. She has always been fascinated with rodeos—and cowboys—so it's no surprise that her first book features one of these strong, silent men. A winner of the Romance Writers of America Golden Heart Award, Leanna lives with her strong, not-so-silent husband in Irving, Texas. Newly married, Gary and Leanna are still honeymooning with their babies—a black Shih Tzu named Muffet and a blond one named Belle.

Dear Reader,

I won the lottery! Well, not really, but that's what this past year felt like. In four months' time I sold my first book to Silhouette, got married to the most wonderful man and won the Romance Writers of America Golden Heart Award. As a romance writer, I can only compare writing and selling my books to falling in love—scary and wonderful all at the same time.

Finding an editor for my story ideas was like getting a date for Saturday night. Like it's said, you'll meet the right man or editor when you least expect it. When Silhouette called to buy *Strong, Silent Cowboy*, I trembled inside like the moment Gary knelt before me, slipped a ring on my finger and asked me to be his wife.

Finally, the story and characters I had created found a home, much as I had with my new husband. My hope is that in reading this book you will experience those exhilarating, breathtaking emotions of falling in love. How can you not love a tall, rugged cowboy whose tough-as-leather exterior guards his tender, aching heart?

Sincerely,

LeAnne Wilson

Chapter One

Kirk Mann walked through the long row of metal pens, feeling like a doomed man on his way to the gallows. The syncopated jingle of his spurs accentuated his slight limp. He slapped his cowboy hat low on his brow, steadied his gaze and squared his shoulders.

The bloodred sky gaped like an open wound along the Texas horizon. A skittish calf bawled. The smell of sweat and manure enveloped Kirk with a sense of belonging, and the dust strangled him with memories.

Cowboys loitered along the corridor, heads bent as they rolled ropes, stretched muscles and cinched saddles. A few old-timers nodded as Kirk passed. Kirk tipped his black Stetson, but kept his focus and moved on, his destination the last chute on the right.

Through the pipe rails, he stared at his nemesis. Cold eyes returned the glare. The Brahma, black as

Zorro's mask and deadly as a two-edged sword, had been appropriately named after the *bandolero*.

A chill pierced Kirk, and sweat trickled along his hairline. His fists clenched. His pulse throbbed at the scar on his temple, reminding him of the pain this bull had caused him so many months ago.

A hand clamped down on his shoulder. He turned toward Smiling Sam Allen and relaxed. This fellow bull rider had been Kirk's friend long before the wreck and was one of few people on the rodeo circuit who knew the full extent of his injuries.

"Looks mean, don't he?" Sam jerked his chin toward the bull.

"What's the b-b-b—" Kirk clenched his jaw and concentrated on the word he wanted to say "—b-bounty up to?"

"Nine thousand and something." Sam ignored the stammer and slapped his leather gloves against the top rail. Zorro lurched, kicking the side slats and rattling his temporary cage. "Nobody's ridden him successfully since you. Guess that kind of money might tempt even you to ride him again," Sam joked.

"Yep." Someday, Kirk thought. Someday soon.

In the midst of his urgent need for revenge, an enormous sense of relief washed over him. The conflicting emotions confused him. He'd never backed down from a fight or cowered to a rank bull. Rubbing the dampness on the back of his neck, he realized the accident had changed him. And he wasn't sure he liked that.

"Hey, Sam, Kirk." A barrel racer sidled up to them. Kirk vaguely recognized her suntanned face, but her name slipped out of reach. "How're you feeling?"

"O-k-kay." His throat tightened with the effort to control the stuttering. He shifted his weight to his good leg, and the ties of his chaps clenched around his thighs.

"You gonna ride tonight, Kirk?" She looked expectant.

He nodded and crossed his arms over his chest.

"He drew Dustdevil," Sam answered for him.

Silence stretched between them. Kirk had nothing to say; he needed time alone to prepare for his ride. However, the young woman hesitated as if reluctant to leave.

"Well," she said, "I guess I'll see y'all around..."

"Sure, Donna, good luck tonight." Sam grinned.

"Same to you." Her gaze swerved to Kirk. "Glad you're back. And good luck."

He nodded, the tension easing as she led her iron gray gelding down the corridor.

"She likes you." Sam's voice sounded as rough as the rope he coiled in his hands.

Kirk shrugged. What did it matter? If she ever heard him talk, really talk, heard his halting stammering speech, then she'd change her mind.

His friend elbowed him in the side. "So, ask her out."

A shadow of annoyance darkened Kirk's face. He ached for the good old days when he'd been quick with a pickup line and eager to ride the devil for eight seconds of heart-stopping excitement. But now, things had changed.

He hooked his thumb in a belt loop and asked, "How?"

"Like you used to do. Just ask."

"That s-s-simple, huh?" He stared down his friend, who glared back with as much determination and stamina as a wild mustang.

"Sure." When Smiling Sam couldn't win the standoff, his face broke into a broad grin. "Heck, if I managed to lasso the prettiest barrel racer, then I bet you can round up one for yourself. Why, you used to be the Casanova of the rodeo."

Kirk almost laughed. Almost. If the pain in his gut hadn't ripped through him like a jagged knife he would have doubled over with a howl of laughter. But he hated this game, the one where friends and family pretended nothing about him had changed. If it hadn't, then why did his insides twist into a corkscrew of defeat?

"You know what the p-p-problem is," he said, his voice resonant with emotion. "I sound like P-P-P..." He paused and closed his eyes for a second. He pressed his lips inward then exhaled. "Damn." He tried again. "I sound like P-Porky Pig."

Sam dug the toe of his boot into the dirt floor. "Nah, it's not that bad, Kirk. It sounds worse to you, is all. Man, any of these girls would love to go out with you. Come on, give it a try."

"No." The word came out soft but held a note of conviction. He wouldn't humiliate himself. Not like that. His gaze veered toward the bull in the chute. If he tried anything, it would be to ride this beast to hell and back once more. "I've got other things to d-d-deal w-w-with now." He bit the words out.

"Like riding this blasted bull?"

Hell, yes! He'd ridden Zorro once. And he could do it again. At least, that's what he hoped. "Yep."

Sam bowed his head, and Kirk knew he understood. They were cut from the same cowboy cloth, unable to back away from a challenge. Kirk's own success had fed an obsession that led him from rodeo to rodeo. Each new event taunted him with another meaner, stronger, bigger bull. He liked the thrill of the moment, the split second of chance.

But now, he wasn't so sure. Was it worth the risk? Was it worth getting hurt again? Getting killed? All for a buck and a moment of glory. It was something he'd never questioned before, and now he couldn't stop thinking about it.

"I know," Sam finally said. "Geena would like for me to quit what with the baby due in a couple months. You know, find something steady, something to help make ends meet at the ranch. But hell..." He grinned. "I just can't yet."

Kirk nodded, knowing exactly how his friend felt, and he respected Sam all the more for not kowtowing to his wife's demands. A man had to do what a man had to do.

"I thought your brother knew somebody that could fix your speech. Ain't she a schoolteacher or something?"

"I s'pose." He shrugged, remembering the arguments he'd had with his brother about speech therapy. Already he felt like a failure, no need to feel less than a man, too. He certainly didn't need some pretty schoolteacher to teach him how to talk. Before the accident he'd spoken fine, and he would again. "I don't need it."

"You're up, Kirk." Trey jogged up beside them, his straw cowboy hat pushed back on his head.

Sam nodded and took his position on the opposite side of Dustdevil's chute. Kirk followed, his steps slow as he left Zorro. *Soon,* he thought, *I'll deal with you.*

The cheers of the Friday-night crowd who'd come for the first rodeo of the spring season rocked the stands; his heart pounded out the same frenzied rhythm. Kirk's insides knotted. He raked his spurs down the inside seam of his jeans, making sure the rowels were locked in place. He gripped the top rail with his gloved hands and stared Dustdevil in the eye.

Not an easy bull, but a good one. This bull kicked up a lot of dust and turned to the right, never the left. Best of all, he'd never charged a downed cowboy. Not like Zorro. Still, Dustdevil made for big thrills and sometimes a pocket-change win.

I can do it. I'm ready. As much as he'd ever be. Distracted by the applause of the crowd and the thunder of his own heart, he searched for the courage he'd once had. He'd learned firsthand from his grandpa how to be a cowboy and act tough as nails, with a backbone that could see a man through a twister or a stampede. But every second he stalled separated him even further from the man he used to be.

"Let's go, Kirk." Smiling Sam looked at him over the top of the chute. His floppy excuse for a hat shaded his laughing brown eyes. "This one's ready for you."

Keeping his mind blank, Kirk settled himself over Dustdevil's back, his hands locked on the side bars. The bull rocked the chute. Kirk tried a deep breath, but could only draw a whisper of air into his contracting lungs.

"Ladies and gentlemen," the announcer's voice boomed, reverberating through Kirk with a trembling intensity. "If you ain't been to the Mesquite Championship Rodeo before, hang on to your hats 'cause these next athletes are top-notch."

Sam squeezed Kirk's shoulder. "Ride him hard."

"We're ready for a little bull-riding action," the announcer said, as Kirk wrapped a leather strap around his gloved hand then pulled it tight with his teeth. "This first bull's a mean one, folks, two shades meaner than the devil himself. Give a hand for a local cowboy, returning tonight to the rodeo circuit after a bad wreck on a bull last year."

Kirk blocked out the announcer and concentrated on... nothing. A haze of memories swirled inside his head, and he struggled to keep them contained. His stomach churned, but he kept his face a mask of indifference, jaw set and eyes hard. Flexing his mended right hand, the tendons stretched and scraped against his bones.

"You ready?" Trey asked, his gaze probing. The question swelled between them.

Kirk swallowed, unable to answer. He couldn't think, much less manage any words. He heard his name over the loudspeaker, followed by deafening applause. It was time. *Now!* But he couldn't give the word, couldn't give even a nod. His hand trembled. He gripped the handhold. He looked at his brother and tried to focus, tried to gain strength from him like he had in the hospital. Numbness swallowed him.

"It's no good." Trey's voice sounded distant.

"What's up?" Sam asked.

"Looks like Dustdevil's got a bum foot," Trey lied, his gaze steady on Kirk. "Too bad. Must've bruised it or something."

Shaking his head, Kirk looked to Smiling Sam. "D-d-do it."

"Wait!" Trey gripped Kirk's arm. "It's no good," he whispered, his meaning clear, his words firm. "I'm sorry, Kirk. I won't let you do this. You're not ready."

Already Sam waved toward the announcer, and the next bull rider shot out of the shoot on Dancin' Dirty's back. Kirk pulled himself off Dustdevil and scaled the rails. Anger pulsing through his body, he stalked out of the arena.

Under the full moon, the parking lot looked like a graveyard of pickup trucks and trailers. Kirk gulped air, his heart pummeling his breastbone. He stopped beside a dilapidated Chevy with a dented passenger side and twisted rear bumper.

Behind him, he heard footsteps. He whirled around and glared at Trey. "W-w-why the hell d-d-did . . ."

"You know why." Trey's voice matched the sadness in his eyes. "You weren't ready."

"L-l-like hell." His body shuddered with anger. Or was it relief?

"I saw it in your eyes, Kirk. The doubt. That's not the way to ride, and you know it. It's a good way to get killed."

Clenching his jaw, Kirk struggled to find the words to contradict his brother, but he couldn't. Trey spoke the truth, but not all of it. Deep inside him a dark, shadowy truth lurked. And he knew. Even though he'd never faced it before, he recognized the signs. Fear. Stark fear.

In the past he'd never hesitated before facing anything, whether it was an angry bull or months of rehabilitation. He'd never faltered from lack of confidence. He'd always gone for what he wanted, whether it was a pretty girl or a championship belt buckle.

Now, he'd failed, fallen flat on his face, his pride crushed. He couldn't ride. He couldn't talk. Frustration ripped at his gut. He stood there with his hands stuffed in his back pockets, his head bent, his shoulders slumped. He had no answers. No solutions. Just a hopeless regret and self-contempt.

"Kirk..."

"It's o-k-k-kay." He stayed his brother's words of sympathy with a raised hand. "I'm f-f-f—" he ground his teeth together, then spit the word out "—f-fine."

"Look, there'll be another rodeo, another bull."

He nodded. But would he feel the same way? Would fear gnaw at him? Would he ever ride again? "I have to do it. Just once more. Th-th-that's all. And it has t-t-to be Zorro."

"I know." Trey studied him for a moment then turned away and headed back to the arena.

Kirk watched him go. At this moment he hated himself. Hated the fear. Hated his inadequacy. How could he change it? His brain waded through the possibilities. He knew Trey was right. He had no business riding a bull in his current state of mind. His confidence needed restoring. He needed something to grab hold of, to give him the courage that he'd lost.

Trapped in a body that ached from wounds and a mind that couldn't grasp the words as quickly as it used to, he conceded defeat. If he could only talk...

Maybe given time...

Shaking his head, Kirk knew that wouldn't happen. He hadn't wanted to face it before now. His body had healed, but his damned stuttering remained a bitter reminder. Maybe he should reconsider his brother's suggestion. From the first he'd balked at the idea; it raked across him like steel claws. But if some speech therapist could actually help, then maybe he'd stand a chance to compete again. A spark of hope flickered inside him. Maybe if he could talk normally, then he'd feel more sure of himself. More confident. Maybe then he'd be ready to ride Zorro.

The school bell jarred Shannon Montgomery, shredding her nerves into frazzled wispy threads. She glared at her friend over the bleached-wood desk in her office at the elementary school. She'd known Trey all the way back to third grade in Mrs. Higgins's class. He'd never asked her for a favor such as this, and she regretted her answer.

"No, Trey, I'm sorry, but I can't."

With his cowboy hat pushed back on the crown of his head and one booted foot resting across his other knee, he looked relaxed sitting in her office. "Why, Shannon? I told you he'd pay. What's the problem?"

She took a deep breath then exhaled. "I don't work with . . . adults."

"You mean men?"

Trey's words cut through her like a blunt knife. She stood and tugged her cotton sweater over her rounded hips. Turning away from him, she looked at the one-way mirrored window into her therapy room. Seated in a munchkin-size chair, Kirk Mann stared back at her. Even though she knew he couldn't see her, her insides trembled. She'd learned the hard way to avoid men like him. Men who courted danger. One in her life had been more than enough.

He reminded her of someone from long ago. A painful memory she'd tried to suppress. Tan, tall and rugged, Kirk had the same reckless look about him. A lock of coal black hair curled across his forehead. His shoulders, wide as a Texas prairie, looked hard and sinewy beneath his white button-down shirt. His black Stetson shaded his deep-set eyes, mysterious and smoldering like a banked fire. His starched jeans covered long, muscled legs, ending with a pair of well-worn, cowhide boots.

A cowboy, with more problems than a little stutter. Like his younger brother, Trey, Kirk rode bulls for a living. Shannon figured he had a wire loose in his brain somewhere.

Trey approached her from behind. "Come on Shannon. He's my brother."

"No." She couldn't look at him. And she couldn't go into the reasons. "I can't."

"You mean, you won't."

"Well, yes." She bit her lower lip. It had always been hard for her to say no, especially to a friend in need. But this time she had to. Self-preservation demanded it. It wouldn't do to get involved with someone like Kirk Mann, a cocky cowboy with crazy notions, even in the most platonic sense.

"He's a nice guy." Trey grabbed her shoulders and turned her around toward the one-way mirror. "Just look at him."

She didn't want to, but her gaze riveted to the strong, silent cowboy on the other side of the gray window. He looked like sin wrapped in a hard, lean package, tempting a girl with too much imagination.

The blue door to the therapy room opened, and little Bobby Joe Dooley slunk into the room like a thief in a dark alley. The seven-year-old stopped dead in his tracks when he saw Kirk, his brown eyes wide with uncertainty. Shannon saw Kirk smile, a friendly, devastating smile, and nod hello to her most troubled student.

"I've got to go," she told Trey. "It's time for my next student." She knew Bobby Joe didn't like strangers, and he didn't yet feel safe in her class. She headed for the door that connected the two rooms.

"Wait!" Trey followed her. "Give me a break here, Shannon. Kirk needs your help. He's got no confidence, not since the accident."

She shook her head. She'd heard it all before. An accident! Please! She knew better. "It wasn't an accident. An accident is something you have no control over. He got on that bull of his own free will, and he paid the price. Don't ask me to sympathize with that."

Trey's eyes darkened with hurt, and she regretted her harsh words. He'd almost lost his brother a year ago, and she knew the slicing pain of loss.

Her face flushed with remorse. "I'm sorry, Trey. I didn't mean that."

He shrugged. "No, you're right. It's not like a drunk driver rammed Kirk's truck or something. He chose to do it. Just like I do every Saturday night. But that doesn't make his pain any less."

"I know that."

"Do you?" He crammed his hands into his back pockets. "The last few months have changed Kirk. He's just not the same anymore. He won't talk. He can't ride. He won't date. He's lonely. His confidence is shattered. I thought if he could...you know, talk better, then maybe—"

"He'd be able to pick up girls? Gain some confidence?"

Trey's mouth quirked with a half smile. "Maybe. But also, I'd have my big brother back."

She sighed, knowing a little confidence could boost Kirk's spirits and possibly help alleviate some of his speech problem. A lack of self-esteem caused most stuttering problems. But she also knew the problem could have resulted from his head injury. "You might be right," Shannon agreed. "But that doesn't mean his problem can be easily or completely solved."

"I'm not asking for a miracle. It's not that bad really. But if he could regain some confidence then he'd be the same here..." Trey placed his hand over his heart. "Where it counts."

She hurt for her friend and his brother, she truly did. But she couldn't take that kind of risk ever again. "I'm not the one to help him," she said softly. "There are a lot of speech therapists around. I'll check and see if I can't find you someone else."

Trey's eyes narrowed, then he finally nodded. "I guess if that's the best I can get."

"That's the best offer I have today."

"Let me know when the bids get better." He winked.

"Oh, you." She plastered on a smile and opened the door, ready to greet Kirk and little Bobby Joe. Her withdrawn student always took every ounce of energy out of her, and she never thought her efforts did any good. She took three steps into the room, then stopped. She blinked with disbelief.

Bobby Joe sat on Kirk's lap, his body nestled against broad shoulders, reading whisper-soft to the cowboy. The contrast between man and boy made Kirk seem even larger, and at the same time, gentler. Her student looked more vulnerable. Shannon's heart ached to help him. The words of Dr. Seuss came in a halting fashion, but they sounded sweet and clear to her. Bobby Joe had never read for her, never spoken more than a few words at a time.

"Your furn," Bobby Joe said, his voice barely above a whisper, his tongue mispronouncing the sounds with a decided lisp. He looked up at Kirk and pointed to the page.

Kirk shook his head. "Nah, you g-g-go ahead, cowboy, you're d-doin' fine."

"Are you gonna see Miss Montgomery for speesh?"

"Yeah, I don't t-t-talk so good."

Bobby Joe frowned. "Me, neither. My daddy says I sound like a sissy."

Kirk raised the boy's arm and pinched the tiny bicep between his thumb and forefinger. "Sissies don't have muscles like this. I think you're pretty tough."

"You do?" A rare glimmer of hope lit up the boy's face as he stared up with awe at Kirk.

"That's right. Takes guts to admit you need help. And courage comes from here." Kirk pointed at the child's chest.

Surprised by the sweetness of the exchange and by Kirk's sensitivity, Shannon's heart contracted. In the last minute, she'd learned more about Bobby Joe than in the past three months of therapy. All because of Kirk. Something about this cowboy frightened her. Was it because he reminded her of someone from long ago, reckless and carefree? Or because he seemed so different?

"Read some more," Kirk prompted, and Bobby Joe continued the faltering recital of rhyming words. When he finished the page, he glanced up. His eyes widened at the sight of his teacher, and his lips clamped shut.

Kirk rubbed the top of the boy's blond head, ruffling his hair, and the corner of Bobby Joe's mouth lifted in a tentative smile. Amazed, Shannon couldn't move or speak.

"That was real good reading there," Trey said, stepping into the room.

"It sure was," she echoed. "Did you make a new friend, Bobby Joe?"

The child's gaze dropped to his scruffy tennis shoes. Kirk lifted him off his lap, set his feet on the floor and handed him *The Cat in the Hat*. The boy scampered toward the far wall of bookshelves.

Slowly Kirk rose to his full height, and Shannon realized he stood even taller than Trey. His wide shoulders blocked her vision of all but him.

"This is Shannon Montgomery." Trey's hand at the base of her back pushed her toward Kirk.

The cowboy tipped the brim of his hat forward, and his steady gaze burned her like a hot, searing laser. "Ma'am."

"It's..." she squeaked, cleared her throat and tried again. "It's nice to meet you. I've heard a lot about you over the years."

His steel gray eyes shifted to Trey then back to her.

"You lived with your grandparents, didn't you?" she asked.

Trey answered with a nod for his brother.

"Well, um..." She owed him an explanation, a reason she couldn't help him with his speech problem, but the words jumbled together in her head. "Trey was telling me, well, that you need some help. Uh, you see, I can't—"

Trey interrupted. "She said that she's—"

"Glad to do it." Shannon stole the discussion back. Beneath Trey's quizzical gaze, her cheeks warmed. Why had she changed her mind? What had possessed her? "I mean...well..." She understood then that the reason lay in Bobby Joe. If this long, tall drink of water could lure her student into a conversation, then he had redeemable qualities. "I'll do my best to help you out. I can't promise anything, but..."

"I'd r-r-r—" His jaw locked tight, set in a hard determined line. She caught a glimmer of despair in the cloudy depths just before he squeezed his eyes shut. When he opened them again, he'd covered his frustration with an icy mask. "I appreciate it."

She placed her hand on the arm he'd crossed over his chest. A tender touch, she'd learned, often helped ease a student's anxiety. But it did little to soothe her flustered frame of mind. Her nerves leapt, sending jolts of apprehension along her spine. She'd never been so moved or felt as fragile as she did now with her hand against his bulging bicep.

"Let's take it one step at a time," she managed to say, "and see what happens."

His smile lit his eyes with a magnetic glow that warmed her from the inside out. And somehow she knew she'd stepped over the edge, taken the plunge and jumped off the bridge into very deep water.

Chapter Two

The heat in the narrow hallway pressed in on him. Kirk paced in front of a garden of construction paper tulips taped to the blue door. Tension knotted his shoulders, and he shook his head at his own foolishness. He'd been in some kind of physical therapy on a regular basis for the last year, most of it painful and almost always essential to his recovery. How could speech therapy be that much different—or difficult? Why did his nerves coil like a lariat?

He glanced at the wall clock and paced for the next four minutes, his mind racing. When her classroom door opened, the little ruffian he'd met the other day raced out and barreled into him. Kirk pulled the boy up short. "Hey, there, B-B-Bobby Joe."

The kid's features contorted with alarm. Recognition lit up his dark brown eyes, and his mouth relaxed into a tentative smile. "Hi," he said in a barely audible voice. "Where's your f-f-fat?" He shook his head, and his lips reformed the word. "Huh-at?"

Kirk grinned and pulled it from behind his back. "A cowboy shouldn't wear his hat indoors. It's not polite. At least that's what my grandma taught me." He ruffled the boy's blond hair. "How's your reading coming along?"

He shrugged. "Okay."

Behind Bobby Joe, the door opened wider, and Shannon stepped into the hallway. When she saw him, her expressive eyes widened. "You're here."

He nodded and couldn't keep from staring. She looked professional and formal in her green dress with her wavy brown hair bundled up on top of her head. Beside the door, he read her name, Ms. Montgomery, in pink block letters. *Ms.* made him think of a sophisticated career woman with a bit of a hard edge. But with her luminous hazel eyes and sweet smelling hair, she presented a different image. He'd seen her smile once at that kid, and he wondered what it would feel like to receive such a disarming gift.

Kirk swallowed hard. He thought he'd been nervous before, but as soon as he saw Shannon his steely composure melted into sweaty palms. How could he possibly think she could help him? She'd only make his stuttering worse.

Shrugging, he tried to make light of the situation. "Just swapping howdys with B-B-Bobby Joe."

The kid looked at him for a moment, as if he wanted to talk some more, but ducked his head. He skirted past them and scurried down the hall.

"He talks to you." Shannon's voice held a note of awe.

Kirk watched the kid disappear around a corner, wondering what she meant. "Yeah, I g-g-guess he does." He liked kids, and this one needed a friend. Like a swift kick to the gut, he wondered if he'd backed over some school rule and gotten off on the wrong foot with Ms. Montgomery. "That's ok-k-kay, isn't it?"

"Of course," Shannon said. "I mean, it wasn't an accusation. I just meant..." As if something had stunned her, she shook her head. "I'm sorry for keeping you out here so long." She stepped back toward the doorway, her composure falling into place. "Come on in, Kirk."

This is it. His stomach knotted at her professional demeanor, but he nodded and entered her classroom. Amazed by the myriad of crayon-colored pictures, smiley face stickers and stacks of games, he stopped in the middle of the gold carpet and waited for her to sit first. She settled herself into a tiny, blue plastic kid's chair, and he sat across the table in an identical one, his knees scrunched up halfway to his chest. He felt like the Jolly Green Giant. Everything looked small and dainty, better suited for Shannon's small hands and pint-sized kids.

"I appreciate your help," he said without a stutter. He'd practiced that over and over. "M-M-Ms. Montgomery," he stumbled over her name, feeling her gaze on him. Feeling ignorant as a schoolboy, he cursed himself.

"Please, call me Shannon." Her lips curved slightly, and her smile somehow reassured him. "We don't need to be formal here."

He nodded. "Shannon." Amazed that he didn't stutter, he grinned. "I'm Kirk."

"Yes, I know." Her eyelids flickered as if she felt ill at ease. "Sorry I ran a little long with Bobby Joe."

"No problem. What's w-w-w—" He clamped his jaw tight.

Most folks when he stammered and stuttered shuffled their feet, coughed or glanced away, but Shannon waited for him to continue, her face calm, her hands crossed on her lap, her gaze resting on him. Her easy manner acted like a soothing tonic on his nerves.

He imagined the word he wanted and tried again. "What's wr-wrong with Bobby Joe?"

She hesitated. "I really shouldn't discuss my students."

"Sorry." He splayed his hands on the table, the cool texture as smooth as her response. "I shouldn't have asked."

"That's okay." Her lips lifted into a half smile. "You seem to have a way with him. What's your secret?"

"Secret?"

She smiled, that heartwarming smile that charmed Kirk clean down to his cowhide boots. "Yeah. He talks to you. To everyone else, he won't speak at all." Her smile faded, and the warmth vanished like the sun behind a cloud. "Every now and then," she continued, "we can get him to whisper."

Wanting to offer some sort of insight into the child, but only knowing his own reasons, he offered a suggestion, "Bobby Joe's embarrassed, I g-g-guess." He fisted his hands in an effort to quell his stuttering. He knew all too well the humiliation of not being able to share easily with others, locked in a lonely world all by himself.

"I know." She leaned forward, interest sparking her eyes. He stretched his legs out, brushing her foot with his boot beneath the table. Kirk jerked away. A pretty blush rose on her cheeks. Breaking eye contact with him, she said, "I'm curious about how you got him to talk the first time. That's the most I've ever heard him say."

Baffled, Kirk shrugged. "He just started t-t-talking."

Her brow knit into tiny troubled lines. "What did he say?"

Rubbing his jaw, Kirk remembered how his worries had distracted him that day last week. "He came in and just stood there, g-g-gawking at me. I said hi. That's all. And he asked me if I was a c-c-c—" Hating the way he sounded, he closed his eyes and concentrated. "C-cowboy."

He opened his eyes, expecting to see Shannon's hopeful expression while he struggled through yet another sentence, but instead she looked pensive, as if she hadn't noticed his blunders.

"Hmm. Interesting," she said. "Guess he likes cowboys."

From her tone of voice, Kirk wondered if she had another opinion of the breed.

"Well, enough about Bobby Joe." She reached for a manila folder. "Let's get busy. I got the medical report you sent. That was some accident you suffered."

He nodded.

"Can you tell me about it?"

He shook his head. "I don't remember much."

She gave him a whisper of encouragement. "Try."

"I was riding Zorro...a bull." Rubbing his palms against his thighs, he thought back to the rodeo. The smell of dust and blood and the sound of hammering hooves transported him back to a hazy recollection. "My hand got c-c-caught in the r-r-rigging." His body tensed, and perspiration beaded his forehead. He couldn't go into details, he couldn't find the words to describe the pain, the chaos. Rather than accept pity, he joked, "Broke just about everything but my nose."

The warmth in her eyes congealed into a cold stare. She glanced down at the medical reports. "Before the accident you never had a speech problem?"

"Just sticking my f-f-foot in my mouth occasionally," he joked again, hoping to retrieve the easiness that had formed earlier.

"Hmm." She ignored his attempt at humor and focused on the facts. "But after the accident your speech became impaired, right?"

"Yes, ma'am."

She opened the folder marked with his name in black ink. She flipped through several pages of medical reports then raised her gaze to his, studying him with a detached curiosity. Slowly she reached out and brushed her finger across his temple. "This scar."

Her gentle touch made his skin tingle. He shifted in his seat, more uncomfortable than he'd been a minute ago. Self-conscious of the many scars he'd accumulated during his years on the circuit, he leaned away from her, breaking the contact. He wondered if she dated pretty boys who wore Italian suits, with slicked back hair and perfect bodies. Why was he thinking something like that? He sloughed off the crazy thought like a dog shaking off rainwater. Shannon had not made a pass toward him, but her caress had made his brain freeze and his tongue tie into knots.

"Is that from the accident?" she asked, her voice calm and velvety smooth as a rose petal.

He nodded, unable to answer.

"Did the bull kick you there?" Her voice wavered. She shaded her eyes beneath a shutter of black lashes.

Most women thought bull riding too rough. He figured Shannon was no exception. Such a delicate, sweet teacher probably didn't want to imagine the hell he'd been through with Zorro.

Finally he shrugged in answer to her question. "Sure. He k-k-kicked the heck out of me. But I don't know what exactly caused this." He rubbed the scar, feeling the raised welt that made a jagged line from his temple toward his eye, and erased the memory of her caress. "Could've been the b-b-bull or the side r-r-rails of the arena. Anything."

She drew her lower lip between pearl white teeth and crossed her arms over her chest as though she'd just caught a chill. He sensed her distance—like a wall had risen between them. She surveyed him with a narrowed gaze as if she used a magnifying glass, analyzing, speculating, gauging with a scientific eye. Her friendly manner had vanished, leaving in its wake a professional demeanor that chilled him like a wintry breeze. Irritation stiffened him. He was a man, not a specimen, not an experiment. Over the past few months, he'd been poked and prodded enough. He didn't want special treatment, nor pity, just help and a little understanding.

But Shannon seemed so prim, so damn proper with her back straight and her hands clasped in her lap. He wanted to grab and shake her until her composure wavered, and . . . what? Kiss her? The idea surprised him yet appealed to him all at the same time.

He took a deep breath to calm himself. Okay, he admitted, he liked her looks. But he'd seen attractive nurses in the hospital. They hadn't made him nervous. Nor had they made his hormones go berserk. But, for some reason, Shannon did. Maybe her formality made him feel like a clod. That's it, he thought. He just wanted to ruffle her feathers a bit, see her squirm rather than himself. And, of course, a kiss on her lips, smearing the pale gloss, would do just that.

Suddenly an image of moist, kiss-swollen lips entered his mind. He imagined her eyes, sizzling with desire, her body warm and pliant beneath his touch. He pictured her brown hair mussed and tumbling down around her shoulders, her cheeks rosy with the heat of passion, and her starched cotton dress rumpled from his embrace. His nerves jolted like a bolt of electricity shooting through him.

"Is something wrong?" she asked, her brow puckering.

"Uh... No, m-m-ma'am." His throat tightened, and he clenched his fists.

How long had it been since he'd kissed someone, much less been intimate with a woman? Too long, he realized, when his body grew hot. From her cool, appraising look, he figured she considered him a student, a handicapped one at that.

That snuffed out his quick flash of lust.

"Well," she said, breaking the silence with a confident tone that he couldn't match. "I thought we'd start with a few short drills." She picked up a stack of picture cards. "All I want you to do is name the picture as fast as you can."

Simple, he thought, until he looked at the first picture, a familiar fruit. He knew what it was, but somehow from brain to mouth the signal took a detour. A full minute passed before he managed to say, "P-p-pear."

"Good," she said before switching cards. She held up the next while she penciled in his response on a score sheet.

This time he blinked, he tensed, he sweated. He knew what the blasted thing did, what it was used for, but he couldn't pull the name out of his head. He sensed Shannon watching him, waiting for his answer. He could almost hear the seconds ticking off. His hands clenched, fighting for him to find the right word. "Steps. No." He shook his head. *Try! Think! Dammit!* Finally, gritting his teeth to stifle as much of the hesitation as he could, he said, "L-l-ladder."

"That's right." She offered him another smile.

A smile of compassion, pity.

He pushed back from the table, his chair clattering against another as he stood. Why couldn't he say what he wanted to say? Why was this babyish drill so hard for him? Was he stupid? Had he suffered an irreparable head injury?

That gave him pause. It was something he'd never dwelt on. Something he'd ignored. Maybe he had a more serious problem than he'd thought. If so, if he had an injury that would never heal, never allow him to talk right again, did he really want to know? Could he face that?

He paced back and forth, heart hammering against his rib cage. Out of the corner of his eye, he saw Shannon sitting in her chair, watching him. She waited, not speaking, not pushing him. Her calmness accentuated his tension.

This wouldn't work. He had to leave, escape.

Kirk looked like a caged animal, pacing back and forth, his muscular arms tense and his jaw hard. He made Shannon's classroom seem even smaller. Used to instructing children, she wasn't sure how to teach an adult—a tall, lean man who looked powerful, ready to pounce in anger or frustration. He had an animal magnetism that lured and frightened her at the same time.

She'd had a taste of his type once, and her heart had been broken. She wouldn't do that again, especially for a reckless spirit like Kirk who liked taking chances. Part of teaching meant opening her heart, getting involved with each student and caring that they succeeded. She couldn't ... wouldn't let herself care for

Kirk. Any man who willingly put himself at odds with a two-thousand-pound bull was nuts. And she planned to keep her distance.

But she'd promised Trey that she'd try to help his brother, and she would hold to her word.

If Kirk had been one of her kindergarten students, she would have given him an encouraging hug and maybe a piece of candy to help him relax and feel more comfortable. But Kirk would probably think her crazy if she offered him candy. And she'd be certifiable if she hugged him!

She'd touched the puckered scar on his temple, which looked cold and cruel but had actually been warm and inviting. His pulse had pounded beneath her fingertips, and her heart had echoed back the same heady rhythm.

No, she'd learned her lesson and wouldn't do that again.

Maybe a breath of fresh air would serve both student and teacher nicely, give them elbow room so that each time they moved they didn't brush against each other. She needed space to control her outrageous thoughts. And Kirk needed time to control his frustration that had resulted from the simple drill of picture recognition.

At that moment he veered toward the door and paused with his hand on the knob. He turned back, his eyes tortured, reflecting a troubled soul.

Maybe she should let him go. It was his choice. If he didn't want help, then she couldn't do much for him. His dove gray eyes beckoned to her, touched something deep in her core. Something she couldn't explain. Something she didn't want to understand.

"Kirk." She stood. "I think..."

His brow lifted with a question that he did not voice.

"Maybe you have the right idea." She tried to appease his sense of pride. She wouldn't let him know that she thought he was running away. Rounding the table, she walked toward him, unwilling to admit even to herself that her knees felt weak. "I think a walk around the block would be great. I'm tired from sitting inside all day. This will be a nice break."

Kirk stared at her for a long moment, long enough for her to doubt her presumptuous statement. Maybe he did just want out. She sensed a restlessness in him, a tense need she wondered if she would ever be able to meet. Which reminded her of someone who she'd rather forget. Maybe it would be better for Kirk to leave, disappear, then she could forget him and her past. She didn't need this constant reminder. The defenses with which she'd learned to shield her heart drained her of all energy.

Slowly Kirk nodded his agreement and held the door open.

Again she'd been wrong. She always guessed exactly the opposite of what he wanted. Now, what would she do with this cowboy?

He slowed his long stride to match hers, and together they walked along the quiet corridor toward the exit. The students had been dismissed for the day, and classroom doors stood ajar. Teachers graded papers at their desks. Kirk's boot heels echoed loud and heavy against the linoleum floor, emphasizing his slight limp. She didn't even want to think of what had caused that injury. The thought of stampeding hooves made her shudder.

The side door clanged shut, and the afternoon sun greeted them with a harsh intensity. The last school bus pulled away from the curb, grinding its gears and emitting a puff of gray smoke.

Kirk guided her down the concrete steps and over a clump of spring grass toward a sidewalk. With matched solitude, they walked away from the school, away from the tension in her classroom, away from their emotional turmoil, toward a quiet neighborhood with shady live oaks and brick homes.

Shannon's thoughts jumbled together with confusion. Although this walk might help Kirk, her insides quivered with nervous tension. She thought he'd looked large and powerful in her tiny classroom, but walking beside her, his height made her feel even shorter. He looked rock solid, his shoulders wide, his legs long and muscular. She couldn't imagine him ever hurt, lying in a hospital, crippled. Strength exuded from him. The frustration clouding his gray eyes hinted at the only chink in his impenetrable armor.

Last week she'd gone on a date with a skinny accountant, who withdrew into his own shell by nine o'clock. She usually liked the quiet, insipid type—no worries, no thrills. But she'd felt like a bowling ball, round and cumbersome next to him. Kirk made her feel dainty for the first time in a long while, a sensation she reveled in.

Frustrated with her errant thoughts, she quickened her step and focused on a new therapy idea. In the few minutes they'd been walking, Kirk had relaxed. The lines had disappeared from between his brows, and the tension around his mouth had eased.

With his thumb, he pushed his hat back on his head. "Nice w-w-weather."

"Uh, yes, it is." She squinted against the afternoon sun. Beads of sweat dampened her forehead from the exertion, but she wasn't about to slow down. The quicker the pace, the more comfortable she felt. Anything slower would have been a stroll, and far too romantic.

"We may get a little rain by tonight," he said.

Skeptical, she studied the azure sky for any clouds. "Is that the weather forecast?"

"Not the o-o-official one." He ducked his head, but eyed her beneath the shade of his hat. "But it's mine."

"How do you know? There aren't any clouds in the sky."

"True." He grinned at her. "But since the accident, my body's like a b-b-barometer. I can feel it in my bones."

She returned his smile. She knew most patients, especially adults, didn't want sympathy for their ailments. They wanted progress. Kirk's earlier jokes downplayed his own pain, but she read the dull ache in his eyes. "So the good news is that you don't get caught in the rain without an umbrella much."

"Well, I guess if I used one, that'd be true." Kirk tipped his Stetson toward her like John Wayne in an old Western. "This seems to do the t-t-trick." His smile faded with his stutter.

She empathized with him, feeling his anger and frustration each time he stammered. Having listened to him, she thought his speech could be improved. She knew his self-esteem had been wounded just as surely as his body. Now, she needed to find something to give him hope, something he could strive for, believe in.

Still she didn't want to give him false hope. She had to be sure before she made a prognosis. To do that, she needed to analyze his speech even more. Her mind wheeled about and tried to find a different path. Her gaze swept the neighborhood, trying to locate a topic he'd feel comfortable with and one that would get him talking. She wanted to test out her theory. Rodeo brought painful memories, but she figured a cowboy loved the outdoors.

"Tell me about your ranch."

He shrugged, but his eyes lit with enthusiasm. "It's home. Used to be my g-g-grandparents'. We have c-c-cattle, horses, hayfields, p-p-pecan trees . . ."

She waited for him to continue, and when he remained silent, she asked, "Any peach trees?"

He nodded. "Like that one."

She looked across the street. Pink blossoms covered a giant tree, its limbs bent with an unseen weight. "It's pretty."

Kirk eyed her instead of the tree. "Yeah."

Her stomach fluttered in response, not the results she'd expected or desired.

Slowly, he glanced across the street. "I hope a late freeze doesn't ruin its c-c-crop."

Keeping her gaze steady on the tree and away from Kirk, she said, "That would be a shame."

Suddenly he caught her elbow and stopped her beside him. His fingers were warm against her skin. Reluctantly she glanced up at him. The dark intensity of his magnetic eyes startled her. Then he smiled.

"Look up there." He tilted his head toward a telephone pole. Wedged against the wood and wire was a clump of brown twigs. "A robin's nest. Can you see her?"

She nodded, and an idea formed in her mind. They could conduct therapy in the great outdoors where Kirk appeared less intimidated. Much better than her cramped office. He could name objects, and she could help him improve his stuttering, which she suspected wasn't actually a textbook stuttering problem at all. It wasn't a conventional form of therapy, but teaching an adult made her stretch for innovative ideas.

"Ready to go on?" he asked.

She followed his lead and began walking. "Kirk, you seem to know a lot about birds and trees..."

He laughed. "Thought that was the birds and b-b-bees."

Her cheeks grew warm, and she avoided his sparkling gray eyes. "That's not what I meant." She waved her hand toward the peach tree. "I mean, you know names of trees and animals." She hadn't fully tested her theory, but she had to steer the session back on track. "You don't stammer over things that you know."

His brow crinkled. "What about bees? I know what they are. I've been stung often enough."

"Of course, you do. I'm just not explaining it very well." On the verge of a breakthrough, she took a deep breath. A thread of excitement wove its way down her spine. "You saw the peach tree and the robin, right there in front of your eyes. But you had to draw upon an image of a bee in your mind."

She stopped walking. "I don't think you have a stuttering problem per se."

He raised an eyebrow.

"Yes, you stutter," she continued, answering his silent question. It felt odd explaining a condition to a student. She usually worked with a child, praising and encouraging, but saved the official jargon for her lengthy reports and parent conferences. "You stutter frequently but not consistently and not for the classic reasons."

"I don't understand."

"Well, a brain injury, which you suffered and which kept you unconscious for three days, can sometimes jumble your memory. Like a whirlwind tossing things about. Your accident misplaced your memory tapes. It's not that you don't know what things are, it's just matching a name with the image you have in your head. And sometimes that causes a pause in your speech, which frustrates you, so you stutter."

For a moment he waited and considered. A light of hope burned bright in his eyes. "So, can this be fixed?"

"It can be made better."

He scowled.

"Kirk, I told you before, I don't offer miracle cures. But with some work we can improve your recall memory. The problem with this is that it's random. You might stumble over *bee* one time and five minutes later you won't."

He settled his hat low over his brow, his fingers trembling slightly. "Then I'm not b-b-brain damaged?"

His eyes pinned her with a desperation that pierced her heart. She placed her hand on his arm to offer reassurance. Her nerves quivered beneath her skin, but she kept her hand in place to emphasize the truth and soothe his fear. "No, you're not brain damaged."

He breathed a deep sigh of relief.

"Is that what you'd thought?"

"It's crossed my mind. I haven't talked much since the accident, not even to my family, but especially not to g-g-girls. I was m-m-m—" His jaw clenched. "M-mortified."

She gave him her warmest smile. "I understand," she said. "But you don't have to be embarrassed around me. I'm here to help. Okay?"

He nodded and laid his hand over hers, encasing her in a dizzying warmth that spread to the cold recesses of her soul. "You know," he said with a grin, "right now, I'm not nervous. You're easy to talk to, not like other women."

Disappointment twisted around Shannon's heart. Just as she figured, he saw her as a plump schoolmarm type. Pretty women with perfect bodies probably made him stutter like Woody Woodpecker. But not her, never her. She chastised herself. She should be glad rather than irritated. It was her job to be accepting and encouraging. He'd complimented her professionalism. But for some reason she wanted to bat her eyelashes and make him stutter just once.

"What about your girlfriend?" She could have kicked herself for such a leading question. Why had she thought that, much less asked it? For his self-esteem, she told herself. A beautiful girl, a sweet smile, a sexy kiss could do wonders for a man. But the way her stomach flipped upside down told her she lied to herself. "I mean, umm..." she stammered. "Is it hard for you to talk to her? I mean—" God, help her!

"*If* I had a girlfriend," Kirk said in a slow cadence, "I hope I'd be able to t-t-talk to her. That she would be able to s-s-suffer listening to me." He attempted a smile. "But I don't have one n-n-now." He glanced away from her.

"Oh." Shannon swallowed, feeling his acute pain. Was he as lonely as she was? Her heart hammered out an excited pattern that she tried to quell.

"When we first started t-t-today, I was nervous," he said.

Startled by his confession, she asked, "Why?" Her heart paused with hope.

His eyes bore into her for a long, drawn-out moment, burning a hole right through to her soul. "You really don't know, Shannon, do you?"

She sensed that she should back away, turn around and run, but she couldn't. With hesitation, she asked, "What?"

He brushed his fingertip along her jaw, and her nerve endings danced. Her lungs contracted. Her gaze locked with his. Slowly, he shook his head, the same characteristic move he made when he couldn't say what he wanted.

Before she could pull away from him, he looped her arm through his. "Sometimes—" he continued their walk, her numb feet shuffling along beside him "—I feel really s-s-stupid."

"Your frustration is understandable," she said automatically. Light-headed, she blamed the tingling in her limbs on the cool breeze and the late-afternoon shadows shifting along the tree-lined street. "But you shouldn't feel stupid. You're as smart as you ever were."

He laughed. "Some folks would say that wasn't too smart. Riding bulls and all."

She tended to agree but kept her comment to herself. Kirk needed his self-esteem restored, not battered even more. Still, his joke gave her hope. If she concentrated on why he rode bulls, then maybe she'd conquer these peculiar feelings his nearness evoked.

"Why did you ride bulls? I mean, it's not something every little boy grows up wanting to do."

He chuckled, a low rumbling sound. "You're right. I guess what I wanted was to be a cowboy more 'n anything."

"Couldn't you do that without riding bulls?"

"I s'pose." He rubbed his jaw thoughtfully. "Guess it was Trey's f-f-fault as much as my own." He turned her onto another street, heading them back toward the elementary school.

A breeze ruffled the loose tendrils at her neck, and the sun began its slow descent, burning the horizon in amber flames. They passed the playground, where an old tire hanging from an oak branch twirled slowly around.

"We used to go out to my grandpa's every w-w-weekend." His arm tensed, the muscles bunching beneath her hand. "We liked to dare each other. You know, see who could throw a r-r-rock farther, who could run faster. One thing led to another and soon enough we were racing my grandpa's mare and an old gelding across the pasture." He grinned at her. "The first time we went to the r-r-rodeo, well, we knew."

Shannon nodded her understanding. He was a thrill seeker, just like Evan had been. To confirm her suspicions she asked, "It didn't scare you?"

He ducked his head. "Ah, heck, sure I was afraid. But there's just nothing else like it."

She stared at him, surprised at his answer. Evan hadn't been afraid of anything. He'd bragged about his crazy stunts, but never admitted fear. She wanted Kirk to be like Evan, so she could remind herself of that fact every time he made her pulse race. She wouldn't get involved with another daredevil. She wouldn't attend another funeral for one, either.

"But, you know," Kirk was saying, "you mount up. The first t-t-time, I sweated something awful. Everyone was watching—my mom and dad, Trey, all the cowboys. Thought I was gonna be sick right there." His eyes darkened to almost black and his jaw ticked. His voice changed from a jovial tone to a hardened edge. "But I d-d-did it."

Shannon tugged her hand away from Kirk's arm as if she'd been burned. Every time she learned more about him, her heart opened more to him. And she couldn't allow that to happen. He was as dangerous as the bulls he rode.

She realized then she'd completely forgotten about the therapy session. Instead she'd been fascinated by him, obsessed with comparing him negatively to Evan, absorbed with finding out more about him.

Quickening her pace, she headed for the school, vowing she'd see Kirk only as a student. Nothing more.

Chapter Three

"Relax and breathe." Shannon's voice sounded as soft and warm as the lazy breeze that stirred the willow branches behind Kirk.

The tree bark dug into his back, and he shifted his sitting position, planting his boots into the soft grass and bracing his elbows against his knees. His jaw worked with agitation as he tried to recall the word for the speech exercise, one of a dozen Shannon had drilled him with over the past two weeks. Frustrated, he opened his eyes and tried to relax, but his muscles knotted. Sweat trickled down his brow. His heart raced.

"Maybe we should take a break," Shannon suggested.

Relief trickled through him. He nodded and stared up at the turquoise sky, the sun singeing the horizon with its golden radiance. Yet even the serene setting in the park couldn't counteract the pressure he felt every time he stammered. He watched a squirrel scamper up the knotted trunk of a live oak and wished he could live as carefree a life. Before the accident, he'd never worried much, but the time in the hospital had made him reevaluate his life, his priorities, his goals. Things had changed. He had changed.

"Kirk?" Shannon asked, caressing his thoughts with the reminder of one of his new goals—to slow down. No more living life on the edge, he wanted a future. "I lost you there for a minute. What are you thinking?"

His gaze focused on her, and he released the air he'd trapped in his lungs. "About how things change."

"What do you mean?"

Stretching his arms out in front of him, he flexed his fingers. "How one s-s-second can change your whole life. One minute I was a bull r-r-rider. Doin' pretty well at it, too. And the next I was laid up in the h-h-hospital for months." He pulled a leaf off a willow branch and rubbed it between his fingers. "It made me rethink a lot of things."

Her gaze looked solemn with a flicker of pain in the hazel depths. "A brush with death can do that to a person." She seemed to hesitate over *her* words. "Even if you're not the one who almost died."

Her grave tone of voice puzzled him, hinting that she'd experienced something devastating. But what? "What happened?" He paused then asked the question gnawing at him. "Did you lose s-s-someone close to you?"

She shrugged and avoided his probing gaze.

Her casual attitude didn't fool him. As a cowboy he knew how to hide his feelings with a lazy smile or a joking comment, anything to cover nerves or fear or embarrassment. Shannon's hesitancy to talk intrigued him. He wanted to press for an answer, learn more about her, but he altered the course of the conversation just slightly. "What changed for you?"

For a moment she stared at nothing, as if she remembered something she'd rather forget, something she wanted to put behind her. "I decided some things just weren't worth the risk."

He leaned back on his elbow. "Like what?"

She shook her head. "It doesn't matter."

He started to disagree, then regretted having pushed her into a corner. His own memories haunted him, and he wouldn't force anyone to face a painful experience again.

"Enough about me," she said in a lighter tone. "We were talking about you. What did you learn while in the hospital?"

Eager to make her feel more comfortable, he relented. He took a deep breath before opening the door to his own past. "A lot. It gave me t-t-time to think. About my life, the things I'd done. And hadn't done. But most of all, I guess it made me slow down. Take my time." He chuckled. "Of course, when I stutter, all that goes out the w-w-window."

"That's understandable." Her soothing voice calmed his accelerated heartbeat. The evening sun filtered through the thin white clouds with a hazy residue of soft yellow light that highlighted her brown hair with blond strands. "Just remember what we talked about last time. Do you think it's helped any so far?"

"Well," he said, "maybe. I haven't really t-t-tested myself." As if he again stood in the rodeo arena, the intensity of the lights making him sweat, his insides twisted as the anger returned, remembering how he'd frozen when that barrel racer approached him. Frustration raked over him like sharp spurs.

Shannon touched his arm, drawing him back to the present. Her fingers felt as soft as rose petals against his skin. He was beginning to like her gentle reassurances. Too much. Slowly his tension eased.

"It's okay," her voice comforted him. "You are doing better."

He knew she was right, but he couldn't seem to stop the anger and frustration that overwhelmed him when he felt vulnerable, like a blubbering idiot. "I g-g-get so angry at myself."

"I know. It's natural. Try and be more patient with yourself. There's no hurry. Remember what we talked about? When you start to stutter, stop. Don't rush, don't push yourself. Take a deep breath and try again. The more you tense up, the more frustrated you'll get. It'll only accentuate the problem."

He nodded and pushed his hat back on his head. He watched her pluck at a blade of spring grass, twirling it between slim fingers that looked as delicate as their touch. Her easy manner and encouragement had sparked a hope, a belief that he could speak normally again.

Over the last week he'd made a few improvements. Around Shannon, he no longer felt like his insides were being ripped apart when he stuttered, but in front of others his stomach clenched with anxiety each time his tongue stumbled over itself. He knew he still had a long way to go.

She shifted her position on the grass and stretched her legs out in front of her. Her skirt formed a canopy over her legs, hiding their shape from him, but his imagination conjured up sexy images all on its own.

A bee buzzed around her, circling her head. Alarm widened her eyes. He waved his hand to shoo the bee away, and it flew toward a gardenia bush, landing on a plump white bud.

Shannon smiled at him then glanced at her watch. "It's getting late. Maybe we should stop for the day."

"Sure," Kirk agreed, tired from the earlier exercises.

He stood and held out his hand for her. Tentatively she placed her hand in his grasp and let him help her to her feet. He held her hand a second longer than necessary, enjoying the warmth of her smooth skin against his callused palm. She felt small and fragile, making him feel protective.

Her eyes met his for a brief moment, then widened with surprise. Awareness rippled between them. She glanced down at her prim shoes. He breathed in her light, airy perfume that reminded him of honeysuckle. If only she would touch him as a lover, rather than as a teacher.

He felt like a schoolboy with a crush on his homeroom teacher. He'd grown accustomed to her hand upon his arm as she encouraged him through a difficult drill, and the brush of her fingers across his hand as she soothed his frustration. He'd responded to her touch, growing easier and more comfortable with her each day. But he'd also realized his body responded naturally to her, as a man to a woman.

She lowered her lashes, a pink hue crept up her neckline, staining her cheeks, and she pulled her hand away from his. She dusted off her skirt and pretended that the second before hadn't sizzled with something Kirk knew was desire. He arched his back, easing the kinks out of his tired muscles.

Not yet ready to hit the road for home or leave Shannon, he asked, "Mind if we w-w-walk through the park first, before I have to drive all the way back to the ranch?"

"Um..." She glanced at him then her eyes scanned the park. "I guess that would be okay."

"You don't have other p-p-p—" He paused, breathed and concentrated on the word he wanted. His gaze met Shannon's as she waited patiently for him to finish. "—p-plans, do you?" he asked, probing to see if she had a date. He'd thought more and more about whether or not she had a boyfriend. He'd asked Trey for any information, but his brother didn't think she dated much. Kirk couldn't understand why, but he was glad she didn't.

"Oh, no. I have plenty of—" She stopped and looked at him again. This time he read the realization in her eyes—she knew he'd tried to see if she had a boyfriend, in a roundabout way. With a slow blink, she shuttered her emotions.

She never finished her sentence. Picking her way through the wildflowers, she walked toward the jogging trail. They passed a bed of red tulips and pink geraniums. "How long a drive is it? To the ranch, I mean."

"About an hour." He smiled at the way she'd changed the subject, pleased she was available.

They fell into an easy step, his long stride shortened to accommodate hers. Their shadows mingled together across the grass, almost like a dance, swaying and moving as one. Their hands brushed once when he limped, and he thought about holding it again. But she moved away and pressed it against her middle. Her wariness reminded him of a skittish colt, which he knew how to handle—with patience.

He wanted to get to know her better and spend more time with her. In order to do that, she'd have to learn to trust him—and he could tell from her hesitancy—to trust herself. For her to give him a chance, he'd have to take a risk he hadn't been willing to take in a long time. He'd have to reveal himself, his successes, failures and dreams. Her encouragement over the past couple of weeks had proved to him that she would be accepting and understanding of his feelings. It would pave a path for her to trust him in the same way.

"You own your grandparents' place now?" she asked.

He nodded. "They left it to me and Trey in their w-w-will."

"Didn't you stay with your grandparents a lot growing up?"

"Yeah. Grandpa needed help. And I'd been having trouble in s-s-s—" he looked across the park at the el-

ementary school and found the word he wanted
"—s-school."

"With your grades?"

He laughed. "No. Just boy stuff. Making trouble.
I'd seen the p-p-principal's office a few too many
times. Dad traveled a lot, and Mom couldn't
c-c-control me very well. So, Grandpa took me in
hand." He rubbed his backside. "Taught me a lesson
or two with a hickory s-s-stick down at the barn."

The surprise in her eyes made him laugh even more.

"Oh, nothing bad," he explained. "Nothing I
didn't d-d-deserve. He set me on a straight path, that's
for sure. Didn't take any of my p-p-pranks, as he
called it. I really liked it at the ranch. I worked hard,
but it kept me out of trouble. So, I went to school
there, while Trey stayed here in M-M-Mesquite."

"I guess that's why I never met you before. I knew
Trey from school, but you were never around."

He nodded, wondering if she would have shown an
interest in him way back then when he talked better.
Was that fair? After all, she was a speech therapist.
Surely a stuttering problem wouldn't prejudice her
from being attracted to him. He'd seen awareness
flicker in her eyes, but he'd also sensed an uneasiness
about her, a signal that she had raised her defenses.
But why?

"Tell me about it," she said. "The ranch, that is."

An idea formed. "Maybe you should come see it for
yourself."

She paused only for a moment then said, "Maybe.
We could have one of our therapy sessions out there

sometime. You can show me the place and all the things that you're familiar with.''

Hope swelled inside him despite her making the visit an "official" one. Part of gentling a reluctant filly was letting her get to know and trust you. And he wanted Shannon to know him. Gesturing toward the playground, he led her across a grassy knoll. "I'd like you to see my home.''

As they cleared the crest, swings and a metal slide came into view. A waiflike child sat on a tilted seesaw, his legs drawn up to his chest and his chin resting in his hands. When they were still several yards away, he recognized the kid who wore an old faded baseball cap that was too big for his head.

"Look who's here," he said to Shannon. Recognition dawned in her eyes. Kirk pressed his finger to his lips and motioned for her to tiptoe behind him. With Bobby Joe's back toward them, he must not have heard them, for he didn't turn around when they approached.

"H-h-hello!" Kirk wobbled the other end of the seesaw.

Bobby Joe jumped, grabbing the sides of the long board. He whirled around, and his brown eyes widened until he recognized Kirk, then a smile tugged at the corner of his lips.

"Hi, there, Bobby Joe," Shannon said. "What are you doing out here all alone?''

He shrugged and looked back at Kirk, tipping the seesaw with an invitation. How could he resist the plea for attention in the kid's forlorn brown eyes?

"Ok-k-kay, let's do it." He straddled the weathered wooden board. The red paint had long since peeled, leaving only a faded reminder. His boots disappeared in the weeds that the gardener had forgotten to cut beneath the seesaw.

Bobby Joe grinned, dimpling one cheek, his eyes lighting with excitement. He positioned himself on the other end.

Kirk jounced the boy up and down. The seesaw squeaked in protest, but laughter bubbled out of the small boy in abrupt spurts as he held on to the metal handle. Kirk noticed out of the corner of his eye that Shannon smiled at them both, and he felt the glow of her enthusiasm light a spark inside him.

Bobby Joe's tentative laughter pulled him back to the present. A soft breeze ruffled a tuft of the boy's hair that peeked out from beneath his cap. Kirk wondered why Bobby Joe suffered? What made him so sad?

"Do you live around h-h-here?" he asked.

"Yeah," Bobby Joe said in a soft voice that Kirk had to strain to hear.

A row of brick homes along the alleyway lined the edge of the park. The houses were small but neat, each with a fence encasing the backyard in privacy. Middle America at its best, Kirk thought. "In one of these houses?"

Bobby Joe's gaze lowered, and he stared at his hands that gripped the handlebar. "Uh-huh."

Kirk glanced at Shannon. Their gazes met, locked and held. At that moment, a closeness, born of concern for this little boy, formed between them.

"Bobby Joe!" A shrill voice called from behind Kirk and raised the hair on the back of Shannon's neck.

The boy's shoulders tensed and lifted nearly to his ears. Before Kirk could brace his legs and balance the seesaw, Bobby Joe leapt off. The other end bobbed and weaved, and Kirk's end thwacked him on the butt. He dismounted like he would a horse and stared after Bobby Joe, who raced toward the woman that Shannon recognized as his mother.

She waved toward Mrs. Dooley, but the gesture was ignored.

"Hurry up, Bobby Joe, before supper gets cold." His mother stood in a garage doorway, a bare yellow light illuminating a battered Plymouth behind her. With her hands planted on her hips, a scowl darkened her face. "I don't have all night to wait on you."

"That's his mother." Shannon shaded her eyes from the setting sun.

"Doesn't seem very f-f-friendly," Kirk said.

Bobby Joe glanced over his shoulder at Kirk just before he disappeared inside the house.

"Maybe she thought we were strangers." Shannon watched the garage door close. The brown paint looked fresh and new, but the grass around the edge of the house needed mowing. By all appearances it seemed like a nice, normal family home. But something was wrong.

She'd met Mrs. Dooley twice. The first time, when Bobby Joe was enrolled in speech, his mother had been cordial and understanding. The second time, when they'd met to discuss Bobby Joe's lack of progress, Mrs. Dooley had been distant, aloof and guarded. Had something happened at home? Had something changed?

Prickles of concern rippled down Shannon's spine. Frightened by her own thoughts and not liking their direction, she pondered other possibilities. As a teacher she had a responsibility to find out what troubled her student. No matter what, she would try and help him.

"He's a sad k-k-kid," Kirk said.

"Yes, he is." Chilled by the prospects of what could actually be wrong with the child, she wrapped her arms around herself.

"You're w-w-worried, aren't you?"

She nodded, and slowly her gaze slid toward Kirk. The setting sun silhouetted his hat and cast a shadow across his face. His eyes flashed with a dark intensity, but he didn't frighten her. His anger connected with hers, touched her, strengthened her courage. He obviously cared about Bobby Joe as she did. She knew Kirk wanted to help, too.

At that moment she realized Kirk was a good man. His heart empathized and hurt for others' suffering. He understood their pain, having experienced it himself.

She'd seen a glimpse of his character when Bobby Joe had read to him that day at school. The tenderness in his eyes and the gentleness in his touch had both hinted at his true self, disproving the image she'd concocted of a reckless cowboy.

At first, his size and daredevil desires had overwhelmed her, warned her to stay away. Now, his power and strength seemed sheltering, a safe haven, a place she could go for comfort and help. With concern about Bobby Joe rising in her, she needed him to assure her that her conclusions were wrong, that her imagination exaggerated the circumstances. She didn't want to believe that anyone would harm a child, but even her short time in teaching had made her aware that a dark reality existed.

Kirk affected Bobby Joe in a way no one else at school had been able to. The two had connected and become friends. Whether it was because they both shared a speech disorder or because they sensed each other's pain, Shannon didn't know. But this strong, quiet man had insight into her withdrawn student. Maybe with his assistance she might help Bobby Joe.

"Yes, I'm worried," she finally answered. "He's not a typical seven-year-old. What do you think about him?"

Rubbing his jaw, his fingers rasped across his five o'clock shadow in a lazy motion that contradicted the tension in his body. "I understand him, I think."

That wasn't the answer she'd expected. "How so?"

"Well," he said, adjusting his hat. "It's kind of hard to explain. I told you earlier how I wanted to be a c-c-cowboy. It represented f-f-freedom to me. Maybe that's why Bobby Joe liked me from the start." He shrugged, looking uncomfortable in the role of hero. "I liked the feel of riding my horse across the open p-p-prairie. The outdoors. I didn't feel stifled. I felt free."

"What did you need freedom from?"

"My f-f-folks mostly. They were good people, don't get me wrong. But they were overworked. And I guess I demanded too much attention. But they didn't understand." His hands clenched at his sides, then he stuffed them in his hip pockets. "They said I couldn't ride bulls." He paused, pain etched plainly on his face in the lines bracketing his wide mouth. "So did others."

"Why? Because they didn't think being a rodeo cowboy would make a good living?" she asked, intrigued by his smoky eyes that looked troubled with memories.

"Nah. Everybody said I was too t-t-tall, too big." He ducked his head. "See, bull riders are mostly small. Good athletes with quick r-r-reflexes. It wasn't that I was a k-k-klutz. I was just so dang tall. No one thought I could do it." He shifted his weight from one foot to the other. "And I believed them."

"I never thought I'd meet a man who wanted to be shorter."

Kirk chuckled. "Well, I wouldn't say that. Unless, of course, it made me a better bull rider." He touched her elbow, and they started back toward the school. "But I've done o-k-k-kay."

They crossed the street and stepped onto the sidewalk. The sun slipped behind the school and bathed the brick in a red glow. All of the windows along the building were dark now, blinds closed and doors locked. In the parking lot, only Kirk's truck and her Toyota were left, a mismatched pair of an oversize black four-by-four and a miniature white hatchback.

"Back then, I got really down," he said in his slow drawl. "There's nothing worse than wanting something but thinking you're not g-g-good enough."

"Goes against the American dream," she agreed.

"Yep. What I needed more 'n talent and d-d-determination was s-s-someone to b-b-believe..." He closed his eyes, and his steps slowed. He struggled for the words, a tick in his jaw revealing the pressure he put on himself. When he opened his eyes, anguish permeated the gray depths, and he touched his chest. "In m-m-me.

"My grandpa did though. He told me I could do whatever I set my mind to whether it was being a d-d-doctor or ridin' a loco b-b-bull." A slow smile lifted the corners of his mouth, relaxing his tense muscles. "He helped c-c-coach me, drove me to rodeo after rodeo. Cheered me when I won and encouraged me when I was tossed on my butt. H-h-he believed even when I didn't."

"And you think that's all Bobby Joe needs?"

His gaze bore into hers, twin slivers of steel determination. "Everybody needs someone to believe in them."

"I hope you're right." She couldn't discount his idea, and she prayed his instincts were right. "You were able to connect with Bobby Joe. No one else has. And believe me, there are a lot of teachers at school who believe in him and want to help. But it's not always easy, piecing the puzzle together."

She stared up at him, his hat forming a dark halo around his head, rimmed by the red glow of the sun. She hadn't figured Kirk out, either. One minute she thought he was like Evan, and the next Kirk proved her wrong by saying something that confused or intrigued her. She wanted to know more about Kirk, about the man who could punch a hole in her defenses. Of course, she assured herself, understanding him would better equip her to help him. But was that her only motivation?

He stopped beside her car and waited while she dug in her purse for keys. When she glanced up, keys in her grasp, she caught him studying her. A nervous flutter tickled her insides.

"Who believed in you?" he asked, his voice deep and raw.

Her hand shook, jingling the keys. She pressed them against her middle. "What do you mean?"

"Well, for you to become a teacher. Who made you believe you could do it?"

A wisp of a smile touched her lips as she remembered her reasons for choosing education as a profession. It hadn't been as much a decision as a calling. "My little sister."

Kirk smiled and leaned against the car door. His wide frame made the car seem even more compact. "Tell me about her."

Not used to talking about herself, she hesitated. The normal desire of keeping to herself, bottling her feelings inside, never materialized. Somehow Kirk drew her out of her shell with his gentle probing and eager smile.

"There were four of us," she said. "I was the oldest and Jeanine was the baby. She was born when I was eight." Acutely aware of Kirk's gaze on her, she stared down at the keys in her hands. "I treated her like she was my baby. Sang to her, rocked her. I was very protective of her."

"Like I am with Trey, I'd guess."

"I suppose. The oldest always knows best."

He grinned. "If only the youngest would realize that."

Shannon caught herself laughing. Her smile still lingering, she said, "When Jeanine went to school, we learned she had a reading problem. Not severe, but enough to require special attention. So I used to help her on weekends or after school. I liked helping her, seeing her progress. Mama always said I was a natural born teacher. Maybe she was right, I don't know. But Jeanine made me believe I could help other children."

"How is Jeanine doin' now?" he asked.

Pride for her sister swelled inside her, and she smiled. "She's a teacher, too. With a specialization in reading."

"See, you can help k-k-kids." He tipped his hat toward her. "You've already helped me. And you're gonna help Bobby Joe."

She gazed back at Kirk, understanding his reasoning about what Bobby Joe needed, wanting to believe. In herself. And in Kirk.

Chapter Four

The breeze wafting through the rodeo arena was as weak as Kirk's nerves. The heat pressed in on him. He lifted his hat, wiped his brow with his shirtsleeve, then settled his Stetson down low over his brow. He'd made his decision, and now he had to follow through with it.

No matter how painful.

No matter how embarrassing.

No matter what.

The sooner he controlled his stuttering, the sooner he could conquer his fear and ride Zorro again.

Gritting his teeth, he squared his shoulders and walked down the corridor of chutes, the smell of dirt and sweat and manure as strong as his resolve. He headed toward a horse trailer where a pretty barrel racer stood. Donna. He reminded himself of her name and practiced saying it again and again in his mind. If he could just talk to her, then he'd prove, if only to himself, that he was making progress with his speech. Each step forward meant a step toward his goal.

Shannon had helped him improve, and he'd come to relax around her. But he remembered all too well how he'd reacted the night of his return to the rodeo circuit. His jaw ticked now with frustration. His determination locked into place. If he could talk without stuttering to Donna, someone who didn't understand his problem, then he'd know for sure that he was on his way to recovering, not just his speech, but his confidence.

And that was crucial if he wanted to ride Zorro or any other bull again.

His gaze narrowed. The shadows of evening fell long in the darkened corridor. On the other side of the rails, the arena lights blinked on, like stars in the night sky. He focused on Donna, his steps, despite his limp, never faltering.

The barrel racer leaned back against her trailer, one booted foot propped on the running board. She could have modeled any brand of Western clothing. Between her fingers she rolled a piece of straw. As he approached, she glanced up, expectancy in her bright smile.

"Donna." He nodded, pleased he'd managed that much. With that one word spoken without a stutter, his confidence took root.

"Hi, Kirk." She grinned and brushed her long ponytail off her shoulder.

"Could ... I mean ..." His jaw clenched.

She blinked, her gaze probing.

He fisted his hand, tightening his grip on his determination. He could do this. He made it a chant in his head. Donna shifted, waiting, watching.

"What t-t-t..." he sputtered like a machine gun. He clamped his jaws shut.

Her smile faded. Her eyes grew wide. She stared at him as if he'd walked up in only his underwear.

His throat convulsed. Still determined to get through this, he focused on what he wanted to say. Sweat trickled down his back. He tried again. "W-w-w..."

"Would...?" she suggested too loudly.

He shook his head. His gut twisted.

"What...?" she asked, as if he'd gone deaf.

He cursed himself. This wouldn't work. He tossed her what he hoped was an apologetic look. She stared back at him, her brow wrinkled, her jaw agape. He couldn't do this. He couldn't talk! His stomach clenched in a hangman's knot. Humiliation radiated from him, making his face hot, his ears burn. Silently wishing her a good day, a good life, he touched the brim of his hat. Slowly he turned away.

"Hey, Kirk?" she called after him. "What d'ya wanna ask me? Is somethin' the matter?"

Ignoring her, he headed for the bulls. Disgust made his steps heavy. Defeat made his shoulders slump.

Again, he'd taken one step forward only to fall two steps back. Why couldn't he talk to a pretty girl? Why couldn't he talk at all?

He could, he knew. He talked to Shannon. She was pretty, with her wide hazel eyes and thick, wavy hair.

Sure, she'd made him nervous at first, but then he'd relaxed, his tension easing. Something about her soothed him. Maybe it was that she didn't get nervous when he stuttered.

Taming his turbulent feelings, he closed his mind to the embarrassing episode with Donna. It was a mistake, he realized. Maybe he'd tried too soon, before he was ready. Just like he'd tried to ride in the rodeo too early.

Still, he had to believe he was making progress. He *had* to trust in himself.

If only he could.

Rubbing the tense muscles along his neck, he saw Trey studying Zorro. A wave of apprehension rolled over him. He quickly forgot Donna as his focus narrowed on the bull and his brother's upcoming ride. He stepped beside Trey and clapped him on the back. "You ready to r-r-ride?"

Trey grinned. "Ready as I'll ever be."

Kirk hoped so. "Watch him," he warned, eyeing the black bull. Zorro butted his head against the chute and snorted. "Son-of-a-gun likes to turn a hard right just out of the g-g-gate. Be careful."

"I'll be fine."

"Watch your grip. Don't wrap it too tight where you can't get loose." That sage advice came from hard experience.

"I will," Trey assured him.

"Don't ever t-t-take your eyes off him, even when you dismount. He's bloodthirsty." Kirk knew this bull. He knew his brother. And he knew what could happen. Watching the black bull's massive shoulders flex, he remembered the savage strength in those muscles.

"I know, Kirk." Irritation made Trey's words crisp, but his blue gaze warmed with understanding. "I can ride, you know."

Kirk nodded.

"Hey," Trey grasped Kirk's shoulder, "don't worry about me."

"That's my job, little brother." He managed a tight smile and looped an arm around Trey's shoulders.

"Well, this is my job tonight. I drew the bounty bull." He slapped a rope against his thigh. "We could sure use the money for the ranch."

Kirk agreed, giving a slight nod, but he couldn't take his eyes off the bull's broad shoulders and blunted horns. He couldn't forget how he'd been stomped, and he prayed for his brother's safety. Was a pocketful of cash worth his brother's life?

He didn't have the answers, and the questions bothered him. He'd never asked them before, and he didn't want to now. Shrugging, he pushed them out of his mind. This was Trey's decision. Not his. Not now.

Trey gripped the top rail and rattled the cage. Zorro tossed his head and snorted. The motion brought an onslaught of jumbled images. The hot searing lights. The loud grunts and moans. The stabbing fear.

"You gonna help me in the chute?" Trey asked.

Pulled back from painful memories that burned his gut, Kirk nodded. "I'll be there."

A while later Kirk stared across the chute at Trey. His brother's focus fixed on the bull as he wrapped his glove tight around his wrist. Kirk knew the concentration it took to ride, knew the discipline needed to keep all feelings at bay, knew the determination that Trey must be drawing strength from now. He'd had all that once, too. But he'd lost his edge.

Below them, Zorro heaved and stamped his hooves and kicked. The rodeo had swung into high gear and the biggest event was seconds away. The dark night held on to the heat from the day. The air hung like wet socks, making Kirk drip sweat.

"He's in an ugly mood," Sam Allen said from his perch.

Kirk shot him a look. He gripped the top rail until his knuckles turned white.

"I meant Zorro, not Trey." Sam laughed.

Chuckling, Trey swung a leg over the rail. "Well, he's gonna be a lot meaner, once I best him." He balanced over the bull and slapped his straw cowboy hat low on his brow. His profile looked stark, his nose sharp as a knife's edge, his jaw hard as granite. He gripped the handhold, eased himself onto the bull's back. "Let's do it."

Heart pounding in his chest, Kirk nodded and waited for the announcer to call Trey's name. His lungs contracted as the seconds ticked by. He stared at his brother, cold fear settling in the pit of his stomach. Kirk breathed in the pungent odor of the bull as Zorro rocked the chute, his muscles bulging and heaving—a ton of exploding energy.

A rumbling, earth-trembling, stands-rocking noise drew Kirk's attention. The crowd cheered, clapping, yelling and stomping, for Trey. An eeriness crept through him. A year ago they'd cheered for him on this same bull. It had been a good ride. But the dismount had been ugly. He'd seen a videotape of how the bull had dragged him around the arena, his body flailing like a wind-whipped flag.

A shiver trailed down his spine as if an ice cube had been dropped down his shirt. He would ride Zorro again, not today, not next week, but soon. It was as inevitable as the shoot-out in the O.K. Corral. He'd ride, not for the money, but for himself, to resurrect his pride and prove to himself that he still had what it took.

Kirk stomped down his hesitations and squeezed Trey's shoulder. "Tame him."

"Will do." Trey laughed, a nervous sound. The metal pipes of the chute rattled with the bull's riotous motions. Kirk helped steady his brother.

"This here Brahma's what we call a bounty bull," the announcer said, not yet turning over the spotlight to the bull-riding event. "With each cowboy he bucks off, his bounty goes up. The first cowboy that can stay on for eight long seconds will find a nice hefty sum waiting in the winner's circle. Tonight, he's worth just over ten thousand bucks." An exclamation rose from the crowd. "It'd sure make this local cowboy smile. Give a hand for Trey Mann!"

Zorro bolted. His hooves crashed against the steel rails. Kirk's insides knotted. His gaze met Trey's. The question lingered between them. He needed to know that his younger brother was ready. Ready to tempt the devil.

With a smile and wink Trey answered him. "Okay, let's go!"

The latch slammed open. The gate yawned wide. The bull lurched sideways into the arena. Zorro kicked twice. His back bowed and twisted.

A flashback of bone-jarring pain assaulted Kirk. He remembered the buzz of the timer, the thrill of beating the bull and the roar of the crowd's cheers. Then everything had gone wrong. Pain rocked through him, his muscles remembering every bruising second.

A disappointed "ah-h-h" brought Kirk back to the present. The bull dumped Trey on his butt. A dust cloud swallowed his brother. His hat lay tossed by the wayside. The clock on the scoreboard showed three seconds.

Kirk held his breath, his heart racing in his chest, his muscles twitching. Zorro circled around, lowered his head and charged one of the rodeo clowns. His horn caught the clown's overalls and ripped them. The clown made a show of almost losing his trousers and leapt into the barrel. The crowd laughed with relief.

Kirk scowled. He knew firsthand the damage those horns could do.

The other clown waved his floppy hat and urged the bull toward the opening at the end of the arena. But Zorro had ideas of his own. He trotted around the railings, staring at the crowd. His hooves kicked up little dust clouds behind him. Cowboys along the rails pulled their legs up out of the way of those horns. When the bull finally spotted the open gate and headed through it, the crowd breathed a collective sigh of relief and Trey leapt down from his perch to retrieve his hat.

The crowd gave him a hearty cheer.

"Did a fine job there, cowboy," the announcer said.

Trey gave a disappointed wave and bent toward his hat. Before the gate closed on Zorro, the bull stopped, turned around and faced the lone cowboy. Butting his head against the gate, he reentered the arena. The crowd gasped. Trey whirled around, leaving his hat in the dirt. Kirk's heart stopped.

The bull pawed the ground, churning up the red dirt. His tail switched. His sides heaved.

A deadly silence filled the arena. The crowd waited. Kirk tensed, poised on the edge of the rails. Trey stared at the bull and backed toward the wall of the arena, each step slow and deliberate.

When Zorro charged, Trey scrambled backward. But the bull was too close. Zorro ducked his head, aiming his horns for Trey. As the bull gained on his brother, Kirk jumped off the rails. Pain stung his bad knee, but he ran forward, waving his hat and whooping.

The Brahma skidded to a halt and turned his gaze on Kirk. The bull lowered his head and cut Kirk off, moving between him and the rails.

Blood pumping through him in a frantic rhythm, Kirk eyed the bull and took a step back, then another toward the far side of the arena behind him.

Wagging his head back and forth, the bull moved forward. His eyes turned red. He bellowed, the sound echoing through the stands.

Keeping the same slow pace, Kirk maintained his distance from the bull. When he reached the middle of the arena, his knee buckled. He caught himself before he fell or stumbled. The bull's eyes rolled, and he

charged. Kirk turned and ran as if the devil himself
was after him, his limp slowing him down. The safety
of the rails on the other side of the arena seemed far
away. The bull was hot on his trail. Blood roared in
Kirk's ears. His heart pounded. His legs churned.
With the crowd cheering him on, he leapt for safety
and hauled himself up on the top rail. Zorro slammed
into the wall, rattling the rails and jarring Kirk.

Drawing an unsteady breath, he calmed his stampeding nerves. Finally Zorro trotted out of the arena,
his head and tail high as if he'd won a battle. Kirk
stared after him, feeling as if he'd been toyed with.
Relief trickled through him, and adrenaline pumped
through his veins. Shaking his head with disbelief,
Kirk caught Trey's gaze across the arena and grinned.

Grim with disappointment over his ride, his brother
slapped the dirt off his jeans and sauntered back to the
middle of the arena to retrieve his hat. Placing it on his
head, he looked back at Kirk and tipped it in tribute
and thanks. Kirk gave him a curt nod of approval, a
cowboy's sign of respect.

When the next bull shot out of the chute, Kirk
hooked his leg over the top rail, faced the crowd and
dropped to the concrete walk. He paused, his knee
aching. Gingerly he tested it by placing his weight on
that leg until he was sure it would hold him.

His gaze scanned the crowd, and he froze.

Shannon.

She sat in the stands, her hands clasped in her lap,
her back straight, her face pale.

* * *

Unable to watch anymore, Shannon stood. Her legs wobbled. Her stomach lurched. Her head throbbed as she walked toward the nearest exit. Why had she come here? What crazy notion had made her think she wanted to know more about Kirk?

He was like Evan, reckless and irresponsible.

A daredevil.

And she needed to stay far away from him.

"Hey, Shannon!"

She turned at the sound of her name and saw Kirk jogging toward her, his slight limp causing a hitch in his gait. She averted her gaze, distracting her heart from feeling empathy. She could imagine him caught beneath the weight of that bull, crippled, limp, bloody. Squeezing her eyes shut, she wished for an easy escape, but knew she'd have to face him and speak civilly.

Near the concession stands, the smell of over-cooked hotdogs made her stomach churn. She swallowed hard and glanced back at him. His brow was creased, but his eyes were alight, making them a pale, misty gray.

"You're here." He smiled.

"Hi, Kirk." She tried to return his smile but failed. She crossed her arms over her chest, feeling a sudden chill deep in her soul.

"I didn't know you liked r-r-rodeo."

"I don't." Her words sounded harsh, but she no longer cared. They created a barrier between her and Kirk. This wild sport was dangerous. And she knew all about crazy risks and foolish men.

Kirk seemed taken aback by her words, his eyes darkening. He pushed his hat back off his brow with his thumb. "Then how come you're here?"

"I...um..." She didn't know if she could put words to the reasons that had driven her here. Driven? Yes, for she'd felt obsessed. Obsessed with Kirk. She wanted to know more about him, understand him. She'd felt close to him, her worries matching his about Bobby Joe, her feelings equalling his, concerning their younger siblings. She'd wondered if Trey and Kirk worked well together as she and her younger sister once had. Now she knew.

Maybe she'd really needed to compare him to Evan. In self-defense, she'd come to the rodeo to put that barrier back between Kirk and her heart. Seeing him a breath away from being trampled, she'd finally succeeded.

Sensing him staring at her, she gazed into his soulful eyes, and her resolve wavered. With one quick glance at the jagged scar along his temple, she squared her shoulders and remained firm. "I guess I was curious. Curious about your former life. Curious to see what would make you and Trey put your lives on the line every time you mounted a bull."

"And did you f-f-find the answer you were looking for?" he asked, his gaze steady, too steady, too calm. But his body looked coiled, as if ready to spring into action.

"No," she said, "I don't understand it at all."

He nodded. "It's a d-d-difficult thing to explain."

"It's crazy," she said, feeling no remorse over her blunt words.

A grin pulled at his lips. "You're right there."

His attempt at humor rankled her. Couldn't he understand? Couldn't he see the senselessness of it all?

A moment of silence ballooned between them, and she struggled with her emotions. She avoided his gaze and tried to figure out how to end the conversation. She wanted to escape into the safety of her own home. Where she'd been content before she'd known Kirk. He unnerved her with his unwavering stare, and she shifted from foot to foot. Dirt had crept into her sandals, and she felt the sandy grit between her toes.

"Most women feel the way you do," he said.

She glanced around her, seeing mamas and their babies with beer-gutted wannabe cowboys standing in line for colas. "Looks to me like plenty of them like it. They sure were hollering for Trey, anyway."

He shrugged. "They think we're like John Wayne, or something."

"I think it's insane."

He dug the heel of his boot in the soft earth. "Sometimes I'm inclined to agree."

"Then, how come you did that...tonight with Trey? You ran in front of a charging bull." She sounded as if she was accusing him of murder. Or attempted suicide. As if Kirk had a death wish. The tremors shuddering through her body made her realize how it had truly affected her. She would have been upset if anyone had done something so foolish, but her explosive reaction stemmed from how she felt about Kirk. Closing off those thoughts, she refused to delve into their meaning.

His brow knitted into a frown. "Trey's my brother. I just distracted the bull from charging him. I couldn't let him get hurt."

"But what if you'd gotten hurt?"

"It happens." He gave her a direct look, his gray eyes steady, unnerving. "It happened before. I survived."

His words struck a chord in her, a chord that made her shiver. "And now you think you're invincible?"

"Nope."

"You'd risk your life—run in front of a deadly bull without a second thought?"

"My first thought was for my brother. And yes, ma'am, I'd risk my life for him. Any day of the w-w-week." His voice sounded rough. "For any reason under the sun."

Contrite, she nodded, figuring it was natural, knowing she'd protect her own siblings if they were in trouble. She should have kept her mouth closed, but the fear she'd felt at seeing Kirk run in front of a charging bull made her angry. Almost irrational.

"See," Kirk said, "he's not just my brother, but he's also my friend. He was there for me when I was hurt. He stayed by my side. He encouraged me. He threatened me." The corner of his mouth lifted in a faint smile. "He believed in me when I couldn't believe in myself." His eyes clouded over with an emotion she couldn't read.

"But it's also more than being brothers and friends. I'd have done the same thing for any of the men out there tonight." He nodded toward the arena, the brim of his hat casting shadows over the planes of his face.

"And they'd do the same for me. Some did last year when I couldn't get loose from Zorro."

He hooked his thumb in his belt loop. Although his stance was casual, his face looked tense, the lines bracketing his mouth deeper than usual. And his eyes. His eyes looked stark, barren, regretful. "I owe them my life."

She had no answer for that. She felt a chasm as wide as the Grand Canyon open between them.

"It's a cowboy code," he explained. "We stick together. Through thick and thin. We trust each other. Look out for one another. Always." His voice cracked with emotion.

At his conviction, unshed tears stung her eyes. Her throat burned, but she refused the temptation to reach out to him, touch him, reassure him. It was the most he'd ever said at one time. And he hadn't stuttered. She knew by the strength in his voice that the words came from his heart, his soul.

Guilt poked at her for the words she'd spoken in haste. Believing meant trust. Kirk seemed to have a far deeper understanding of that.

She'd trusted before, only to have Evan disregard her feelings. And she wouldn't do that again. She couldn't apologize for her own convictions. If only she could take back her words. If only Kirk wasn't bent on self-destruction.

"I guess you don't know what I mean." His brow furrowed. "Maybe it doesn't matter." His voice dropped to a low whisper.

The pain she saw in his eyes tore at her, ripped at her defenses.

"I'll see you, Shannon." He tipped his hat in goodbye and turned to go.

"Kirk?" she said, touching his arm. Her sudden action surprised her. "I'm not sure I understand everything. But..." She became aware of the heat radiating from him, and she pulled her hand away. She pressed her palms together. What had she wanted to say? Why had she stopped him?

"What?" he asked.

"I understand basic respect and trust in relationships. You have that with Trey...and the other cowboys." She twisted her hands together. "I guess cowboys are a whole different breed of man from what I'm used to."

He tilted his head as if trying to understand her. "We're different in some w-w-ways. Same in others. There's more to bein' a cowboy than ropin' and ridin'. Just like there's more to bein' friends than hangin' out together."

She shook her head, unable to speak.

"I'm a cowboy. That's all. That's not bragging, either. It's a d-d-dirty job—" He broke off with a grin. "And I'm not sayin' it as an excuse." His lips curved, and tenderness made his eyes glow like warm coals. "Maybe if you could see what being a cowboy is all about, you'd understand."

"Maybe," she said, "but I doubt it." Still, something inside her made her want to believe whatever he said. She wanted to stifle that impulse, but she couldn't. She found herself waiting when she should have walked away.

"Come to the ranch."

"What?" Startled, she took a step back.

"T-t-tomorrow," he said. "Come to the ranch and see what I do. Every day. Not this." He glanced over his shoulder at the livestock at the end of the arena, then he stepped toward her. His breath fanned her face like a warm, sweet breeze. "I'd like you to see my place."

Stunned by his invitation, she twisted her fingers together. Of course they'd bantered around the idea of holding a therapy session at the ranch, but this didn't sound like that. "Um, Kirk..."

His hand cupped her chin and lifted it until she met his solid gaze. Her body warmed. Her skin tingled. Her heart pounded out a warning beat.

She wanted to pull away but couldn't. His touch somehow reassured and comforted her. Yet at the same time, she felt things she shouldn't.

"Please," he said.

She blinked and tried to think. If she tried to speak, she knew she'd be the one to stammer and stutter. She licked her parched lips. Knowing she should run instead of agree, she stalled for an answer. "For our next therapy session?"

His eyebrows slanted downward and creased the skin over the bridge of his nose. "That's not what I had in mind."

"What did you have in mind?"

He shook his head. "Not for my speech. For me." He touched his chest. "For you."

How could she resist? How could she agree? She wavered, torn by her fear and Kirk's need. She knew he needed her to understand him, believe in him. As his brother once had. But could she? Her mind whirled, confusion jumbling her thoughts. Her pulse pounded in her ears.

"I could come into t-t-town and pick you up," he offered.

"No." The word came out too harshly, and she tempered it, saying more softly, "No, that's all right. I can drive out there." She stopped. What had she done? Had she just agreed?

He smiled, and her questions dissolved.

"That's no problem," she said, deciding at least that way she could leave at any time.

"Then, you'll come?" His eyes gleamed.

"Yes." She barely breathed the word.

"Good." His thumb caressed her jaw. "I'll see you then."

She knew she was in trouble. Big trouble. But she couldn't think of a way to back out now. She would have to cloak herself in her professional demeanor, even though the visit had nothing to do with therapy, and forge her way through her murky feelings.

After all, Kirk was only a student, she reminded herself, only a student. But a tiny voice in her head warned her they'd already become friends, and she already cared for this strong, silent cowboy.

Chapter Five

Pressed for time, Kirk pushed open the back door, hauling the last plastic garbage bag out onto the back porch. The sun glared from its perch in the noonday sky and reflected off the white railing. Anticipating Shannon's imminent arrival, his stomach tumbled over itself.

Trey coughed and glanced up from his task of sweeping leaves off the porch floor, raising the dust as he went. "You sure this is necessary?"

"Yep." Kirk stepped over Trey's pile of leaves and took the steps two at a time, a trash bag in each hand. He limped slightly, his knee sore from his workout the previous day. Without looking back at his brother, he headed toward the barn.

"Must really like her, huh?" Trey called after him with a chuckle.

A smile tugged at Kirk's mouth, but he didn't answer. He whistled a jaunty tune, something he hadn't done since before the accident. His heart felt light and free from burdens.

The sweet scent of gardenias and roses wafted toward him on the cool breeze as he passed his grandma's flower garden. He'd pruned the bushes earlier in the year, and now his efforts had paid off with generous red, pink and white blossoms. He hoped Shannon would appreciate them. Stopping for a moment, he snapped off a white rosebud and slipped it into his shirt pocket, wanting it to remind him of his family's love. He needed the encouragement as his nerves tightened in anticipation of Shannon's arrival.

Kirk continued on to the storage room down at the barn where he hid old feed sacks and trash bags. All morning he'd shoveled moldy scraps of food out of the refrigerator and tossed out old newspapers. Things sure did pile up during rodeo season. Next, he headed toward the corral, his pliers and work gloves in hand. Trey joined him a few minutes later and helped secure the barbed wire. Satisfied, Kirk slapped his gloves against the fence post. He checked his watch, then his gaze followed the drive that led to the farm-to-market road. No sign of Shannon.

"She'll be here," Trey said. "Don't worry."

"I'm not," Kirk replied, irritated at his brother for reading into his every action.

"Could have fooled me." Grinning, Trey clapped his brother on the back. He wiped the sweat off his brow and squinted up at the sun. "I'll go make some iced tea. It's gonna be a scorcher."

Kirk watched his brother walk back toward the house, and his thoughts focused on Shannon. He hoped she hadn't taken a wrong turn. As far as he was off the main highway, sometimes newcomers found it tricky to find his place, but he liked the peace and quiet of country life. He'd been raised with it. Now he needed its calming effects even more than he had as a boy.

The sound of wheels crunching gravel drew his attention. Shannon's white car crept up the drive over the ruts in the road as she eased her way toward him. He waved to her and thought he saw her smile through the windshield. His heart melted a degree. He waited until she parked beside the old gas pump that his grandpa had once painted red. After releasing her seat belt, she climbed from the car.

Her jeans molded over her nicely rounded hips, and her white ruffled top accentuated her ample breasts. Although her cotton blouse was modest, it revealed enough of her creamy neck and shoulders that Kirk wanted to skim his fingers over her smooth, warm skin. Her cheeks looked rosy, her mouth moist and kissable with a light gloss. He forced his thoughts back to reality.

"Hi, Sh-Sh-Shannon." He stuttered, but not from his disorder. He just couldn't think clearly with her near, the sight of her was so enticing.

"Hi." She walked toward him, and the grass cushioned her boot heels.

Glad that she'd dressed in good, old-fashioned country attire, he also appreciated the fact that she looked natural. She was his type of girl, he thought, not gaudy and not too prissy, but with just the right touch of femininity—all in a cozy down-home way.

She smoothed her hands down the tops of her thighs, seeming more uncomfortable in her jeans than she did in her work dresses. "I hope it was okay to park there."

"Anywhere's fine." He closed the gap between them, and her light scent reminded him of the flower garden. "It's g-g-good to have you here."

"Hey, Shannon!" Trey called as he walked toward them from the house. "Look at you, cowgirl." He gave her a quick hug then winked at Kirk. "Never thought I'd see the day that Shannon Montgomery would dress in jeans and boots."

"I've changed since we went to school." She smiled weakly and looped her purse strap over her shoulder.

"Any of my brother's doin'?" Trey asked.

Kirk held his breath and hoped he had influenced her, maybe encouraged her to change her heart about taking risks. But he doubted he'd affected her in such a short time. Had something else changed her, like the accident had changed him?

A pretty blush rose on her cheeks, and she glanced down at the ground. "Well, um . . ." She paused. "I guess a lot of things can work together to make you change. But I wore these old jeans knowing Kirk was going to show me around the ranch. I didn't want to ruin my clothes."

"Well, I like it," Trey said.

So did Kirk, but disappointment sifted through him, not lasting long enough to destroy his hope, but sprinkling a dose of reality on his notions. Shannon was cautious, wary as a frightened doe. Something kept her at a distance. And he wanted to discover what that was and dispel it. But he'd have to go slow, real slow.

"Come on inside the house and we'll get you something c-c-cool to drink," Kirk suggested. "It's kind of hot today for such a long drive." He gestured to the front of the house and followed a half pace behind the other two, his limp more pronounced than usual.

"This is really very nice." Shannon's soft lilting voice came from the living room. Shannon stood on his grandma's handwoven rug, scanning the room.

"It's home." Kirk hitched his Stetson to the hat rack in the hallway. He'd been proud of the way he'd straightened the room, dusting even the baseboards and the ceiling fan. "Hey, Trey, why don't you go get Shannon some iced t-t-tea?"

"Huh?" Trey's blue eyes widened, then brightened with understanding. "Oh." He winked and grinned. "Okay." He headed toward the kitchen. "Shannon, iced tea okay with you?"

"That's fine." She set her purse beside the couch.

"Sugar?" Trey yelled from the other room.

"No, thanks."

Now that they were alone, Kirk didn't know what to do or say. With his insides jittery with nerves, he followed Shannon's gaze around the room, anxiously waiting for her verdict. He saw the room as he supposed she did, dark and masculine, almost like the inside of a log cabin. He opened the curtains, and sunlight slanted across the room and highlighted the bookcase containing his rodeo trophies. The smile on her face faded. A keen sense of disappointment rocked through him.

Hoping for an unruffled-looking stance, he hooked his thumb in his belt loop. "Guess it looks kind of r-r-rough to a g-g-girl, huh?"

"Well . . ." Her gaze riveted to the barbells in the corner. "It looks like a place a man could live in and be happy. I like all the dark paneling and the wood floors. Though it must take a lot of work to care for."

He couldn't think of a reply.

She walked over to the bookshelf in the corner and studied the silver buckles and yellow and blue ribbons. "You won all these rodeoing?"

"Heck no," Trey said before Kirk could reply. He handed a glass of iced tea to Shannon. "Most of them are mine that you're looking at."

"All the t-t-tarnished ones," Kirk said.

Shannon laughed.

Relaxing, Kirk stepped up behind her, noticing that the top of her head came just below his chin, and caught a whiff of the fresh scent of her hair. "I guess Trey w-w-won a few. And these . . . are m-m-mine." Reaching past her shoulder, he showed her the ribbons and awards he'd won in high school, then the belt buckles he'd won as a pro. He wanted her to be proud of him. Touching the cold metal of his last trophy, he said, "This is what I won when I r-r-rode Zorro last year."

"Zorro?" She turned and looked up at him, a question in her hazel eyes.

Memories clouded his mind, but he focused on Shannon.

"The bull that nearly killed him," Trey added.

Her eyes glazed, and her face paled. Kirk noticed her hand shook, clinking the ice in her glass. Why had he ever thought she would be impressed with his accomplishments after seeing her reaction at the rodeo?

She stepped away from him. "Why don't you show me around outside?" Her voice sounded strained.

Discouraged by her lack of interest, he nodded. Maybe he'd bragged too much. Maybe she'd seen enough. Maybe she didn't like his home. What really hurt was that she probably didn't care for him, either. He avoided Trey's curious gaze, grabbed his hat and held the door open for her.

"Are you coming, Trey?" She paused at the door.

"Nah, Kirk can handle this by himself. I've gotta go to the feed store for a while. I'll see y'all later."

Ten minutes later, Trey drove the truck down the drive, and Kirk escorted Shannon around the barnyard. The flower in his breast pocket weighed heavily against his heart. How could she ever believe in him when she was repulsed by what he did? Or used to do? With each passing minute she seemed more distant. Her arms wrapped around herself as if the temperature had suddenly dropped.

He spoke of how he wanted to expand the herd, but it didn't seem to interest her. He pointed out the vegetable and flower gardens, but she remained silent, only encouraging him when he stuttered. And he seemed to do that often with his nerves stretched tight as barbed wire. He couldn't imagine what had happened, what he'd said or why she'd become stoic and icy.

He glanced sideways at her, catching her delicate profile. At a loss as to what to do now, he offered the only suggestion he could think of in hopes that a look into his future plans would show her he was more than guts and glory. "How would you like to see the back pasture, where I'm gonna build my house someday?"

She turned her gaze toward him, and surprise brightened her expression. "Okay. Sure."

"This way." He led her into the dimly lit barn. The scent of fresh hay was strong. He stopped in front of a stall. "This here's Ginger."

His sorrel mare peered over the door, her big brown eyes telling him she was eager for a ride. He opened the stall gate and led the horse by her halter toward the saddles.

"What are you doing?" Shannon asked, hesitancy in her voice. "I thought . . ."

"I'm gonna s-s-saddle my horse. Thought we'd ride over there. It's real nice through the trees, but the t-t-truck can't get through that way." He ran his hand down the mare's nose and cupped her velvety lips. Over his shoulder, he saw Shannon back away. "Don't you like h-h-horses?"

"Sure, I guess . . . but I've never been around them much."

"Have you ever ridden one?"

She shook her head.

"Oh, then we gotta do this. Don't worry, you're dressed for it." His gaze roamed appreciatively over her, and her cheeks grew rosy. "But since you're unsure, we'll d-d-double up. It'll be easier that way."

* * *

Panic inched along Shannon's spine, stiffening her with icy dread. Was it fear of riding or fear of being so close to Kirk? She imagined herself pressed up against him, her back to his front. Bodies hot. Temperatures rising. The way their bodies would rub against each other. Just thinking about it, her body grew warm. Alarms went off in her head, warning her of danger. Too much of a risk for her.

How could she get out of this?

"Maybe this isn't such a good idea." She tried to keep her voice from wavering. The scent of hay and manure grew strong, and she couldn't breathe. She shook her head and found Kirk watching her, his steely gaze intense and boring into her.

He shifted his feet, tipped his cowboy hat back on his head, and hooked a thumb in his jeans. "I kind of made up a p-p-picnic lunch for us." Disappointment etched the lines deeper on his face. "But if you don't feel c-c-comfortable riding, then I guess we could just eat at the house."

For a moment he stood there, one hand resting on the horse's flank. He watched her, and she tried to guard her reactions, her thoughts.

Guilt trickled through her and congealed in her stomach as a cold, solid lump of regret. She hadn't thought he would prepare lunch for her. As a matter of fact, she hadn't thought much about his feelings at all. Not wanting to spoil his efforts at being a generous host, she surprisingly found herself wanting to please him, wanting to see him smile. He had, after all, been willing to accommodate her, eager to put her at ease.

Jittery at her sudden change of heart, she spoke before she could change her mind. "No, that's okay. I didn't realize the trouble you'd gone to. We can—" she swallowed hard "—ride, if you want."

Nodding his appreciation, he gave her a simple smile of approval. Her insides warmed; the cold dread that had been there before thawed. When he'd spoken in jest of his accident, she'd been reminded of Evan and noticed a few similarities between the two men. With Kirk's back to her now as he readied Ginger, Shannon studied him, the hard, chiseled muscles rippling under his shirt, his hands, quick and efficient with the leather.

"Ready?" he asked.

She couldn't answer, but she couldn't back down now. Slowly she stepped forward and surveyed the tall, still horse. The reins looped from the corners of the mare's mouth and rested across her neck, but there was definitely something missing. "Where's the saddle?"

"We'll ride b-b-bareback. Don't worry, I won't let you fall. Ginger's got a nice rounded back." He ran his hand over the smooth hide. "It'll be more comfortable that way than with a s-s-saddle."

"Oh," she managed to say.

"Come on, I'll give you a hand up." He walked his horse outside. The sunlight brightened the mare's coat to a golden red. Swinging himself up onto his mount, he settled himself back toward her rump. "Hand me those saddle bags, will you?"

Shannon found the leather pouches hung over the corral fence and handed them up to him. He placed them over his broad shoulder.

"Okay, your turn." He smiled down at her, his gray eyes bright with enthusiasm.

She stared up at him, unsure what to do or how to do it.

"Just step up on my foot." He flexed his booted foot out before her. "Give me your hand, and I'll p-p-pull you up."

She hesitated. He stretched his arm down toward her, and his eyes beckoned for her to trust him. With a shaky breath, she lifted her foot onto his and gripped his hand. Before she could gasp or blink, he lifted her onto the horse and settled her snugly between his rock solid thighs.

"How's that?" he asked.

"Okay," she squeaked. For one brief second, she relished the little effort it had taken him to hoist her up. He was stronger than she'd imagined. Then the horse shifted beneath her. Shannon panicked and gripped the coarse mane.

"Whoa," Kirk said, his breath caressing her ear. "It's o-k-k-kay. I've got you." His arms came around her as he took the reins. He urged her to lean back against his chest. "How do you feel now?"

All she could do was nod.

He clicked his tongue, his thighs clenched around hers, and the horse moved forward slowly. Still uneasy about riding the horse, she felt secure and protected with Kirk's body encasing her in his warmth.

Each step rocked her against him, her body soft and curvy, his hard and powerful.

She soon forgot about the horse and could think of nothing but Kirk. The feel of his arms. The tangy scent of his cologne. The warmth of his body. A tingling in the pit of her stomach undulated outward to every region of her body in tiny prickles of awareness.

Her body slowly awakened, aroused after a long, dormant, self-imposed sleep. She'd avoided circumstances like this since Evan. Men usually made her uncomfortable, anxious, expectant. Kirk made her feel comfortable, yet at the same time aware. Aware of his every movement. Her senses seemed more acute, tuned to him. A shiver trembled down her spine, and an ache grew deep inside her, a fluttering of need, a whisper of desire.

She paid little attention to her surroundings of the ranch, the lowing of cattle, the whiffle of a horse, the sectioned-off green pastures. Each nerve focused on the sensations that Kirk stirred within her, the way his breath rustled her hair, his arm brushed the curve of her breast, his thighs cupped her bottom.

"Shannon," his voice broke into her thoughts and startled her. He sounded hoarse. "I'm sorry if I upset you earlier. What I said about Zorro and all. It happened. But I'm o-k-k-kay now. 'Cept for this dang s-s-stutter."

"Why would I be upset about that?" She tried for nonchalance, but even she heard her voice rise sharply with denial. She wondered if he was as disturbed by their closeness as she was. Somehow that idea made her even more uneasy, even more hungry for something she could not let herself have.

"Well, I s'pose it's not very pleasant c-c-c—" His body tensed, and the muscles in his arms bunched.

She didn't have to see his face to know he clenched his jaw. She could imagine the agony in his eyes. In response to his frustration, she touched his forearm, encouraging him to continue. After a moment he relaxed and tried again.

"It's not very pleasant to t-t-talk about. It happened. And it's over." He paused, as if weighing his words before he spoke again. "Sometimes I have a hard time believing I'm not the same person."

She warned herself that she shouldn't ask, she shouldn't even care, but she wanted . . . no, needed to know. Just yesterday, she'd searched for the common link between Kirk and Evan. And she thought she'd found it. Had she been wrong? Was Kirk different? Finally, unable to hold back the question, she asked, "How so?"

"Well . . ." The muscles in his arms flexed, and she felt the tension in him build, the tightness in his abdomen against her back, the hardness of his thighs. "Remember how I told you about the first time I rode a bull. How s-s-scared I was and all." His heart throbbed against her. "That's what has ch-ch-changed."

"You're not scared anymore?" If that was so, then she could equate him with Evan and forget about Kirk altogether. It made sense. Once someone faced death, often they no longer feared it.

"That's not what I meant." He sighed.

Again, she'd misjudged him.

"I got over being scared after the first time or t-t-two," he said. "Oh, sometimes I'd get nervous, if I drew a really rank b-b-bull. But most of the time it was a rush. But not anymore." His voice cracked, and with it her heart.

For a long while, he didn't speak. She waited, her breath caught in her throat, her heart hammering. They rode along a narrow path; a canopy of gently waving branches overhead protected them from the hot sun. It sounded like a sanctuary. Leaves rustled in the slight breeze that brought a sigh of relief through the trees. Birds twittered in the distance as they called their mates. Insects buzzed and chirped in harmony. A dense carpet from several generations of leaves covered the ground and softened all sounds, even Ginger's slow, plodding gait. The air smelled fragrant with fresh hay and honeysuckle.

"Before I came to you for help," he said, as they headed up an incline. "I tried to ride again in the r-r-rodeo. I was ready. No, that's wrong. I wasn't. My body had healed, but, heck, my mind's all messed up. I got s-s-s—" He sputtered to a halt.

Without looking over her shoulder at him, she knew he clenched his teeth. Her heart ached for him, as she imagined the foreign emotions he'd felt, emotions he'd never had to face. Wanting to help him through this difficult confession, she placed her hand on his thigh. His heat scorched her, and it took every ounce of self-restraint not to pull her hand away.

"I couldn't do it." The agony in his voice melted her resolve.

She knew that had been hard for this strong man to admit such a weakness, but she considered it a definite plus. A good healthy dose of fear might keep him alive. Could it be that he'd given up the rodeo? Had he come to his senses? Hope soared within her, but a thread of concern for Kirk's self-esteem held it in check.

She knew how he felt—like a coward. She felt that way now, afraid to go forward, scared she'd fall back into something which she'd narrowly escaped a few years ago.

Her mind screamed *Evan,* as a warning to her.

But her heart thundered *Kirk, Kirk, Kirk* in a steady, determined beat, encouraging her to take a chance.

As Kirk's horse crested the brow of a hill, Shannon sighed, her hand still resting on his leg. She felt connected to him—emotionally. They'd bonded as teacher and student. And in another way she refused to think about. The forest of oaks gave way to a meadow. Wildflowers waved in the breeze, their colors forming a paint palette across the lush grassland. The dense woods surrounded the meadow, keeping it hidden and secluded from the outside world. She felt content in their own private world.

"This is it," he said. "This is where I'm going to build my house."

Overwhelmed by the breathtaking beauty, she could only stare. Ginger dipped her head and nibbled on the tall grass until Kirk urged her forward with his knees.

"There'll be a drive along here, leading up to the f-f-front door." When they reached the middle section, he reined to a stop and dismounted. He looked up at her, a yearning in his gray eyes. "Do you like it?"

Unable to speak, she nodded. She imagined a cozy log home with a roaring fire in the fireplace. A home in the truest sense of the word. A safe place. "It's perfect."

He smiled, beaming his pleasure at her approval. His hand touched her knee. "Just swing your l-l-leg over, and I'll help you down."

She followed his instructions, and he bracketed her waist with his large hands, making her feel small. He lifted her down and set her a few scant inches away from him.

"That wasn't so b-b-bad, was it?" he asked.

Unable to tear her gaze away from his, she shook her head, mesmerized by the intensity in his eyes, the deep longing that she sensed. Through her thin shirt, his hands felt warm and callused around her waist. Again, his size astonished her and made her feel petite. His broad shoulders looked too thick for her hands to span, and his muscular chest seemed the perfect size for her head to rest upon.

She tried to think of something to ease the tension building between them. "Are you hungry?"

His mouth curled into a smile. "Yeah."

She gave him a tentative smile, wondering at his husky tone.

He squeezed her waist. "Come on, let's eat."

He spread a checkered cloth over the grass and opened the leather pouches, unwrapping sandwiches, fruit and cheese. Shannon settled herself on one corner of the cloth and nibbled on a strawberry. Her thoughts drifted like the wind, awed by this unique man who loved the outdoors and had a gentle, caring spirit.

"How's little B-B-Bobby Joe?" He took a bite of tuna sandwich.

"About the same." Amazed at his concern for one of her students, she confided in him, "But I've scheduled a parent-teacher conference for next week."

"That's good."

"It should prove interesting."

He nodded and swallowed the rest of his sandwich. "I bet he'd enjoy going to the rodeo. I'll get him a couple of tickets. What do you think?"

Shannon smiled at the generous man beside her. "I think he'd love it."

Kirk ducked his head. His fingers plucked awkwardly at a loose thread in the checkered cloth.

"Thank you for bringing me here," she said, feeling the truth of her words. "And sharing this part of your life with me. It's so different from the rodeo."

He nodded and slipped his fingers into the pocket of his shirt and pulled out a white rosebud, a bit wilted but still intact, and handed it to her. "I'm glad you came."

Taking the rose, Shannon realized she'd changed. She doubted Kirk's accident had altered him but rather enhanced those alluring qualities of tenderness and strength that were already embedded in his personality. The defenses she'd struggled for so long to build came tumbling down around her, which left her heart open and bare to this ex-rodeo cowboy.

Chapter Six

Kirk's hand trembled as he watched Shannon sniff the rosebud. Her mouth curved with a faint smile then faded. Her eyes widened with awareness, as if she sensed what he felt.

He couldn't take his eyes off her, the way the sun lightened her brown hair to a sandy blond and touched the golden sparkles in her hazel eyes. Her smooth, flawless skin looked radiant in the afternoon sun, her cheeks a healthy pink.

"Thank you," she said. A simple statement, rich with meaning.

"You're w-w-welcome." He thought of several lines he might once have used, but the words stuck in his throat. Not wanting to sputter them out and ruin the moment, he realized sometimes words were unnecessary. His meaning lay within the gesture.

"It's beautiful. Is it from your rose garden? The one by the side of the house?"

He nodded, pleased that she'd paid more attention than he'd thought.

"How did a cowboy learn to grow roses?" she asked, a hint of humor lurking at the corners of her mouth.

Laughing, he said, "Not all of us are rednecks."

"I didn't mean . . ."

With a raised hand, he stayed her comment then offered her a smile. "I guess it is a little odd for a c-c-cowboy to take so much pride in a rose garden. But my grandma loved hers. She loved all kinds of flowers. R-r-red roses especially.

"Some of the best times I ever had were helping her w-w-weed her garden." A vivid picture of his grandma came to mind, with her sitting in the dirt, her jeans rolled up to mid-calf, and a wide-brimmed hat shading her eyes. "She used to tell me stories."

Shannon smiled, her eyes glittering. She leaned forward and rested her arm against her knee. "What kind of stories?"

"Oh, lots of different ones. Family stories about my folks or my grandpa. Sometimes she'd tell me about Brer R-R-Rabbit or Pecos Bill. Then sometimes we'd just talk." With his thumb, he pushed his hat back on his head and squinted against the sun's harsh rays. "She'd ask me about school and my friends. She took time to be with me. Something my folks hadn't done."

He looked down at a tiny white scar on the pad of his thumb. "She used to make me pick her flowers every evening to set on the s-s-supper table. Got a few scars from all the thorns. Guess after a while, I learned to be more careful."

She glanced down at the rosebud she still held and stroked the stem with an awed reverence. "She sounds very special."

"Yeah, she was. I miss her and my grandpa a lot."

Her gaze narrowed on him, concern etching a line between her brows. "When did they pass away?"

"A few years back. A car wreck." He remained silent for a moment, remembering the acute loss. "Guess it was for the best. Them going together. They would have been miserable without each other."

Solemnly, Shannon placed the flower beside her on the cloth, brushing a velvety petal with her fingers before she focused on her lunch. With each bite she took, he watched her lips, lush and inviting, envelope a plump strawberry. Pink juice glistened at the corner of her mouth. He wanted to lick it off but enjoyed seeing her tongue dart out quickly and erase all traces.

His insides tensed, and a tremor of desire rippled through him. Did she realize the effect she had on him? He shifted uncomfortably on the blanket, feeling the tightness of his starched jeans.

Concentrating on his surroundings, he tried to ease the hollow need inside him. The tall grass encircling their picnic blanket waved in the breeze, bending and swaying with nature's rhythm. A white butterfly fluttered from a steepled bluebonnet to an unpretentious pink buttercup in search of sweet nectar. Kirk's thoughts veered back toward Shannon.

There was so much he felt and wanted to say, but the words were locked inside his head. Would he ever be able to free them? Frustrated, he ate the rest of his lunch and polished off the last of the grapes without putting voice to his thoughts.

As the minutes ticked by, her silence began to weigh heavily on him, and he started to doubt himself. She'd never shown much interest in him, other than teacher to student. Had he made a fool of himself giving her the rosebud? Had he crossed an invisible line?

Maybe it was something he'd said. He thought back to what he'd revealed while they'd ridden Ginger together through the seasoned oaks. He'd wanted Shannon to know him better, thinking she'd learn to trust him eventually. Had his plan backfired? In a moment of recklessness, he'd unbandaged his own festering wound—his cowardice.

Could that have been a mistake? Women didn't want to know a man was afraid. They wanted a man, especially their own special man, to be fearless, forceful, proud. He had none of those qualities anymore. He'd been broken, his limp but a symbol of how his self-esteem had been crippled in the accident. If only he could take back his words. . . .

"Shannon . . ." He cleared his throat then tried again. "What I said earlier—" readjusting his hat, he squinted against the brightness of the sun "—with the r-r-rodeo and all. It's not what you think. I mean, bull riding is—" He groped for the right word and looked to her for help.

"Scary," she suggested. Her eyes deepened to a pine green. Kirk wondered if it was sympathy, understanding or dismay. He prayed it wasn't pity. "It's okay."

She touched his arm, electrifying his skin with stunning sensations that shot through him, ricocheting around inside him. Her gentle caresses no longer comforted him; they set him on fire, scorching him with her tentative touch. He studied the tips of his boots and fought for control of his body.

He felt naked, baring all his scars, even his soul, like a newborn calf wobbling on unsure legs. What if she rejected him now?

"Everybody is scared sometimes." Her voice had that comforting tone that she often used to encourage him.

But he wasn't relieved yet. He'd grown up with the cowboy code. No cowboy worth his salt ever admitted fear. When he'd ridden bulls, sure he'd been scared, but he'd set his jaw, lowered his hat and took whatever came his way. Like a man. Never complaining. Never whining. And that made him feel even more cowardly now that he'd cast a light on his fear.

Still, he knew Shannon was right. Everyone felt afraid at some time. He sensed no condemnation, no contempt from her, which eased his mind somewhat. "I g-g-guess you're right."

"I know I am." Her voice sounded almost commanding. "If you weren't scared, then you'd be either lying or just plain stupid."

"I must be smarter than I thought," he said with a wink. Cocking his head to the side, he studied her, amazed by her intuitive nature that read him so easily. Like a salve, her words eased his suffering pride. "How come you seem to understand me so well?"

Her hand withdrew from his arm, and he yearned for the return of her warmth. She glanced away, just for a moment, then her gaze met his again, dark with uncertainty.

"What did I say?"

"Nothing." She sounded soft as the flutter of a butterfly's wings. "It's just that..." She stammered into a long pause. "You've been honest with me, Kirk. Maybe it's—" her voice trembled "—time I was honest with you."

He waited, his breath caught in his throat. His pulse hammered against the scar on his temple, a steady but frantic beat. She twisted her fingers together, then splayed her hands against her thighs. Over and over, her palms rasped against her jeans, her knuckles white with tension.

With a shaky breath she said, "I'm afraid, too."

Surprised by her confession he asked, "Of what?"

He leaned forward, wanting to touch her, but not daring to.

Shrugging, she avoided his eyes. "Of a lot of things, I guess. Me...you..."

Her voice cracked, and he reached for her, no longer able to keep himself from touching her. He wanted to comfort her the way she had so often done with him. He cupped her chin and lifted her gaze to his. For a long moment he studied her, helpless against the tears filling her eyes. Like a wound reopening he relived his own pain, his own frustrations, and understood how she felt, how defeating fear could be. He'd waited a long time, wondering why he'd sensed a hesitancy in her, and now he wanted to know why she was afraid of him.

"What have I d-d-done?" he asked, concern lacing his words. "Don't be afraid of me, Shannon. Talk to me."

She took a tremulous breath and pulled away from him. "It's not really you." She sniffed and blinked back the tears. Her eyes looked like a misty forest in the early dawn. "It's what you *do*. Who you are."

Confused, he said, "I'm a cowboy. A rancher."

She nodded. "Yes. But you're also a daredevil. A bull rider."

Her words slammed against him, leaving him speechless.

"Evan was like that," she continued, a faraway look in her eyes. "Not a bull rider, but he lived on the edge. Loved to take foolish chances."

"Evan?" he asked, his neck tightening. He didn't want to know more. But he *had* to know.

She sighed and plucked a purple thistle, twirling the stem, the prickly leaves whirling like a windmill. "My college boyfriend." She looked grim, her lips a straight, thin line, not tender with reminiscences. "He was wild and carefree."

Kirk's hands flexed then fisted. His gut clenched. If Evan had hurt her . . .

"He died." Her voice sounded flat, unemotional, but a single tear rolled down her cheek.

His heart contracted, restricting the hope he'd once had for them. Who was this man that still had a hold on Shannon? What had he done to her? Jealousy inched its way through his veins, leaving him cold with the harsh new reality. Or was it that she still loved him, the loss fresh and tender, that she couldn't bare the thought of becoming involved with someone else, someone who risked his life every week. "You still love him?"

She shook her head, her hair swaying with her vigorous denial. "No. I'm not sure I ever really did."

Relief warmed his blood, but confusion churned his thoughts. With his thumb, he brushed away the hot tear. "Then why this?"

She shrugged, and her chin quivered. "He was my first real boyfriend. When we met, I thought he was so...cool." A hint of a smile tilted her lips. "I was the envy of all the girls. They all wanted Evan. But he liked me. I guess I wanted him to love me. I was infatuated with him, intrigued by him, and I craved his approval. But love?" She shook her head. "I didn't know what love was back then."

"How come you wanted his approval so much?"

Tilting her head, she gazed off, tears still glistening on her eyelashes. "I guess it was like a fix of some kind. I'd never really had a boy pay so much attention to me. And I liked it. And before I knew it, I'd do anything to hold his attention." She sniffed. "Not a very healthy attitude. But I guess pretty common for young women."

Not knowing what else to do, he pulled her against his chest and held her close, wrapping his arms around her, loving the soft warmth of her and breathing in her sweet scent. With her near him like this, he felt like he could protect her. But he'd learned a long time ago that he couldn't shield his loved ones from sorrow.

Resting his cheek against her silken hair, he hoped he could help her cope with her own loss and make her somehow feel secure...with him.

She didn't push away from him. Instead, she nestled her head against his shoulder and tentatively touched his back. He wanted to ask more questions, find out more about her past, but he wouldn't rush her.

With her voice muffled against his chest, she finally said, "He...Evan...killed himself."

Kirk's muscles flinched, as if he'd received a sudden blow. "How? I m-m-mean, why? What happened?"

"He didn't put a gun to his head, if that's what you mean." She sounded cold. "But he might as well have." She took a deep, trembling breath, and a shudder rippled through her. "He liked to ride his motorcycle. Without a helmet." Anger saturated her words. "And, of course, he had to drive at reckless speeds. He lost control one afternoon while he was driving down a highway. And he crashed." Her arms tightened around him, hugging him close as if she needed him to warm her suddenly chilled body, to comfort her, to make her feel alive. "He died instantly."

Realization hit Kirk like a mule kick to the gut. He knew then why she feared him, why she hated what he did. "And you think that's what I do?"

She nodded, her chin rubbing against his chest.

It wasn't the same to Kirk. He wasn't crazy. He wasn't foolish. He was a cowboy, that was all. He did what he was good at, what he had to do. "I ride bulls for money," he said, his voice strong. "To make a living, so I can work my r-r-ranch."

For a long moment she said nothing. Then whisper soft, she asked, "Do you enjoy it?"

Regretful of his answer, he knew she wouldn't understand. He got a rush of adrenaline, unmatched by anything else when he rode bulls, but he wouldn't consider himself crazy, not like her dead boyfriend. But he wouldn't lie to her, either. "Yeah, I used to enjoy it. But I didn't take unnecessary r-r-risks."

She shuddered in his arms, and he knew she disagreed. Could she ever see him as the man he was inside, rather than what he did or used to do?

Not knowing what to say or how to help her, he cradled her against his chest, rocking her in a slow, easy rhythm. She felt warm and soft, fragile as the flower he'd carried so carefully in his pocket earlier. Smelling her honey-scented hair, he waited. Waited for her to make the next move. Waited to see how she would react next.

Her heart thumped against his, their pulses accenting each other's in a synchronized rhythm. With slow deliberation, he stroked her back, long even strokes from shoulder to hip, feeling the narrowness of her waist and the slope of her lower back beneath his palm. Eventually her shallow breathing evened out, underscored by a few snuffles, and she relaxed against him. Her body molded to his, her curves fitting snugly against his hard, lean lines.

He brushed a kiss across her hair, and she pulled away from him. She stared into his eyes, mesmerizing him with her sudden intensity. He yearned to kiss her mouth, her eyelids, her neck, trailing a path along the neckline of her shirt and below. But did he dare?

This was his one chance to try, to take a risk.

He'd taken so many in his life. Why did this one make his insides shake and his mouth go dry?

"Shannon," he said, his voice thick with emotion. He settled his Stetson low over his brow and met her watery gaze. "I'm a cowboy. Plain and simple. I do what I have to do to earn a living. It's not always an easy life. Sometimes it calls for a s-s-sacrifice. I've paid my dues. I've got the scars to prove it. But only God knows what each day holds. When it's my t-t-time, it won't matter if I'm riding a two-thousand-pound bull or a tricycle. I won't have a choice. Neither will you. Neither did Evan."

She glanced away from him, and he tipped her chin toward him and waited for her gaze to meet his again. When it did, he read the hesitancy, the fear in her hazel eyes. He wished he could take it all away, but maybe she needed to face her fear to control it. Just like he had to face Zorro again, in order to go on with his life.

"When it's all said and done, it'll be worth everything if I've made an impact, if I've touched someone in a p-p-profound way. It won't matter then the *if I'd only*s, or *I should have*s. It's what I do with the hours, days and years before, that count, not how or when I die. I want to make each moment worth something. Now."

Grasping her shoulders in his hands, he pulled her to him and kissed her. His mouth landed firmly on hers, not yielding, not compromising. He took a chance that he thought was worth the risk.

A delicious shudder rocked through Shannon's body. She melted against him, all reservations drowning in a pool of desire. Her heart opened to him, and her arms clasped him tighter against her. His words spun around in her head as her senses reeled from his eager kiss.

He tested the seam of her lips with his tongue, tempting her with delicious sensations, promising her all she'd ever imagined. Her lips parted, and her breath mingled with his. She drew in the tangy taste of grapes and his masculine scent. A warmth flooded her body as his tongue touched, stroked and caressed hers. She savored the rough and smooth textures, the deep, wet thrust of his tongue tickling the roof of her mouth.

His kiss gentled, and he teased the corners of her lips with little nips and soft, tender kisses. Then he eased her away from him. His gray eyes smoldered with passion. Her pulse skittered, making her feel jittery.

With alarming clarity, she realized that Kirk had the same traits that had attracted her to Evan, but at the same time he was nothing like him. Maybe she'd known that all along. She'd denied it, fought it in her heart. Maybe that's what had frightened her about Kirk in the first place. She had no defenses against him.

But what did she have to fear? His tender caresses had drawn the poison of Evan's selfishness out of her like salve to a throbbing wound. Around him, she felt whole. With him she felt safe. Beside him she felt cherished.

No longer able to deny her feelings, she knew she wanted him. Wanted him with a deep, urgent desire.

His breath stirred the wispy tendrils along her hairline, and a delightful shiver trilled through her. It was time, time to move forward, time to relinquish the past. What did she have to fear about Kirk, anyway? He was a cowboy, a strong yet tender cowboy. He'd once been a daredevil. But he'd changed. She knew that now. He was wiser, grounded in his convictions, cautious due to his fears.

Her heart thumped faster, and her breath quickened. Before she could question her own instincts, she leaned forward and pressed her mouth to his. His lips felt warm and pliant, softer this time than before, yet firm and solid like his character. She let her lips linger against his for a few seconds, then she pulled away.

She met his surprised gaze. Her insides jumbled together, anxious for more of a response from him. His hands bracketed her shoulders and pulled her closer to him. Her breasts brushed against his chest, just enough to tantalize and tease her. He paused with their mouths but a breath apart. His gray eyes brightened, and he gave her a quick flash of a smile. Then his mouth descended on hers, tempting her with his tongue and with playful nips along her bottom lip. Sighing, she opened to him.

As his mouth mated with hers, she gripped his solid shoulders, holding on to him for balance in her suddenly tilted world of whorling senses. He skimmed his hands down her sides, brushing his thumbs along the tender slopes of her breasts, and her back arched with need.

She longed for him to run his hands along her body in slow, languid caresses, building to an urgent, greedy frenzy. At the same time, she wanted him to touch more than her flesh, she ached for him to reach her heart. Beneath layers of walls, she'd hidden her heart from everyone, keeping it safe and protected from any pain. But she knew that Kirk could touch her there, open her heart to wonderful possibilities. He could make her feel alive once more.

He kissed her again, a sweet promising kiss that both comforted and kindled the desire within her. Still holding her securely against his hard chest, he nibbled on her earlobe and down the column of her neck, licking and teasing her sensitized nerve endings. A dizzying current arced through her, making her toes curl and her world spin.

His hand pressed against her hip, and she felt his urgency, his need. His breath sounded loud, his skin felt damp. She knew then that he wanted her as much as she wanted him. But a tiny wedge of doubt inched its way into her thoughts. Would she be enough for him? Could she match his desire? Would he be disappointed in her?

Her body tensed with apprehension, and Kirk lifted his head. His gray eyes were clouded with passion. "What is it?"

Words wouldn't come. She shook her head, unable to voice her concerns.

"Too much?" He smoothed back her hair and kissed her temple ever so gently, almost reverently. "You're so b-b-beautiful."

Was she? she wondered. For so long, she'd doubted herself, her appeal. It had served to protect her from other men like Evan. She'd never trembled in Evan's arms, never sensed that he valued her as a person, as a woman, a mate. Holding on to Kirk's shoulders, she felt really beautiful. In fact, she'd never felt as lovely as she did now in his arms, basking in his attention.

She swallowed the bitterness of old regrets. Evan had been a mistake. A terrible, painful mistake. But she'd learned from her lessons. Hadn't she? Kirk was different. Kirk was unique. Wasn't he?

"Shannon," he said, his voice deep and smooth. "Th-th-this changes things between us. I don't want to be just your s-s-student with a speech problem. I want you to see me as a man, as your equal."

She understood his need. "I know."

For a long moment he didn't speak. His finger followed a path of light freckles down her arm. "Is that what you want?"

She understood his doubt. "Yes."

"Can you think of me as more than a student?"

"I already do." Her voice sounded hoarse, but sure and steady.

He hugged her close, then set her away from him. He readjusted his cowboy hat. "Maybe we should go on back."

Startled, she glanced at him. Yes, he wanted her, but she knew he wouldn't force her, wouldn't manipulate her into something she didn't yet feel comfortable with. She appreciated his patience and understanding. "Thanks . . . for everything."

He smiled, and the burden in her heart lifted. "My pleasure," he tipped his hat, "ma'am."

After a quick kiss on the corner of her mouth, he stood and held out his hand for her. A few minutes later, with the saddle bags packed and mounted on the horse, they started back the way they had come, down into the cool shade of the trees.

The sun slipped beyond the rim of the treetops, bathing them in a warm, amber glow of late afternoon. The breeze rustled the leaves and chilled Shannon's heated skin. She leaned her head back and rested against Kirk's shoulder as he guided Ginger along the narrow trail. With her eyes closed, Shannon felt the gentle swaying motion and Kirk's breath hot on her neck.

His finger stroked her earlobe then trailed down her shoulder, along her arm until his hand rested on her thigh. Even through her jeans, she felt his warmth seeping into her, awakening the passion she'd denied for so long.

"Shannon?" He squeezed her leg. His thumb brushed against her sensitive inner thigh. "W-w-would you . . . ?"

She waited, anticipating what he would ask her. She covered his hand with her own, offering support.

"I . . . um . . . have to ride in the rodeo on S-S-Saturday . . ."

She stiffened.

"Are you okay?" he asked.

"Yes." Lifting her head from his shoulder, she realized she'd been wrong. Again. "Of course." Why would whatever he did upset her? "So, you're going to ride bulls again?" She tried to sound nonchalant, but her voice quavered slightly.

"No." He hugged her close. "Not next week. I'm sorry if I worried you. I'm riding Ginger in the opening ceremonies."

"Oh." Slowly she relaxed against him.

"I know you don't like the rodeo. And, well, we don't have to stay for all of it, but would you g-g-g—" He tensed, his hand against her side clenching into a fist.

Recognizing signs of his frustration, she took his hand in hers and waited for him to continue, idly stroking the soft hairs on the back of his wrist. Her insides quivered.

"W-w-would you . . . go with me?" he asked almost roughly. His characteristic stammer, the way he stuttered when nervous, touched her deep inside. She had a hard time picturing him as enthralled with the risk associated with rodeos.

"Yes." Her voice sounded still and small in the amplified sounds of the forest. She didn't know why she'd agreed, except that it had nothing to do with rodeos and bull riding. It had everything to do with Kirk.

He sighed, and his tension eased. "Good."

She stroked his palm with her thumb, wondering at his strength . . . at his gentleness . . . all in the same hand.

Rodeo was in his blood, a part of his life. Forever. Even if he never rode bulls again. She would have to accept that. Could she? Could she accept the danger that seemed to flow in his blood?

Chapter Seven

His heart galloped, a frisky pace of exhilaration. Kirk breathed in the lusty odors of rich earth and healthy animals, scents he'd grown used to and now meant coming home. In odd ways the rodeo was his home. It had taken him in as a wayward boy, fed him with dreams, sheltered him from the wrong influences, accepted him as part of a loving family.

Like a thirsty sponge, he soaked up the sounds of jingling spurs, the sharp, brittle crack of hooves against wooden platforms and the loud laughter of a nearby cowboy. Excitement swelled within him like the gray clouds overhead. He was overflowing with enthusiasm, knowing that it wouldn't be long until he would once again take his place with the best bull riders and cowboys here.

Escorting Shannon through the narrow passageway that housed the metal pens and chutes, Kirk walked with his head high, his back straight. His limp felt less pronounced, less of a burden. His injury seemed far in the past, almost a blurred memory.

"Hey, Kirk, you ridin' tonight?" Smiling Sam Allen looped a rope over his shoulder and sauntered toward them.

"Just my h-h—" he paused, made himself relax and continued "—horse." With a wink he glanced at Shannon and kept his hand at the base of her back. "Sam, this here's Shannon Montgomery."

Smiling Sam tipped his sweat-stained cowboy hat. "It's a pleasure, ma'am."

After Shannon greeted the short, wiry cowboy whose grin was as wide as a watermelon slice, Kirk explained, "Sam's one of the best bull riders around. After me, that is."

The cowboy with crease lines bracketing his mouth slapped his hat against his thigh and laughed. "You just keep thinkin' that. Wait'll you see me ride tonight."

"Who'd you draw?" Kirk asked.

"Zorro."

The name sent fear—but also a wild anticipation—coursing through Kirk, stirring his blood with its challenge. He felt ready, ready to try again, ready to challenge his nemesis for the last time. He credited Shannon for helping his confidence grow. Now, he'd blocked all doubts from his mind, concentrating on his need . . . his goal. Nothing would stop him. Nothing, not even the ever-present anxiety, would get in his way. This time he'd overcome it, conquer his fear, ride the bull. He'd drawn the rank bull himself and was scheduled to ride in a month.

"Bounty's up to near twelve thousand."

"Wouldn't mind having that, would you?" Kirk asked. "What with you and the missus having a baby soon."

Smiling Sam's grin blossomed. "Yeah, I'm gonna be a daddy. I'm the luckiest man alive. Can you believe that one?"

"Can't believe Geena's stuck with you this long." Kirk clapped Sam on the back. "Gotta check my mount. I'll be watching you later. Ride t-t—" he relaxed his suddenly tense jaw "—tough."

"Always." Again, Sam tipped his hat to Shannon. "Nice meetin' you, ma'am."

Kirk wrapped his arm around Shannon's waist, and together they walked toward the stalls that held the horses. When they reached Ginger, Kirk saw Trey, stretching and warming himself up for his bull ride. His brother's white straw cowboy hat was set low over his brow in a no-nonsense manner. Kirk gave his brother an encouraging nod, then ran his hand along his horse's backside.

"Did you want to go talk to Trey?" Shannon asked from the stall doorway.

"Nah, don't wanna bother him now. He's got to get his c-c-concentration for his ride. It's bad news if a cowboy isn't ready to ride." He checked the saddle, tightening the girth. "Let's go find our seats. Then I'll come back for the opening p-p-procession."

A few minutes later, in the stands, looking down at the packed dirt floor of the arena, Kirk wedged his way through the aisle, his hand holding on to Shannon's. He handed her a program and a plastic cup of cola, then brushed a kiss across her temple. "I'll be back before you miss me."

"I doubt that." She smiled.

He grinned at her, then felt a tug on his belt loop. Looking down, he saw Bobby Joe seated in the row ahead of Shannon. The little boy's eyes brightened beneath his scruffy cap of blond hair. "Hey, c-cowboy."

The kid grinned, and he poked the broad-shouldered man beside him in the bicep.

The man glanced at Bobby Joe then up at Kirk, and recognition brightened his bloodshot eyes. "Well, hell!" He slapped his hand against his thigh. "It's Kirk Mann." He stood and stuck out his hand. "Glad to meet you. You're one of the best riders around. I've watched you a lot."

Kirk shook his hand, the man pumping his arm like an oil rig. "Thanks." He nodded down at Bobby Joe. "You know this little cowboy?"

"He's my son." His lower lip bulged with snuff. "This the one you was talkin' about, Bobby Joe, that got us these tickets?"

His son nodded, his gaze firmly set on Kirk.

"Well, damn! That's great. We appreciate it. Mighty nice of you. I tell you," the man hooked his thumb in the band of his jeans beneath the overhang of his belly, "I didn't know Bobby Joe was hanging around a real live bull-ridin' cowboy. Reckon you'll be a good influence on him. Bein' a real man's man and all."

Kirk's brow wrinkled. "I surely do hope so. But I'll tell you, Bobby Joe's been a big help to me."

"He has?" The man's eyes bulged.

Nodding, Kirk ruffled the boy's hair. Bobby Joe stared up at him like he was the Lone Ranger or something. Kirk didn't like the role of hero; it made him feel like he'd forgotten to zip his fly. But if the little boy needed someone to look up to in life, then he'd be glad to do his part.

"Want him to grow up tough," Mr. Dooley said, his chest puffed out like a stubborn gelding refusing to be saddled, "quit talkin' like a sissy."

Bobby Joe ducked his head, looking down at his scuffed tennis shoes. Kirk felt the jab of humiliation that he knew the little boy must feel. How could a father be so cruel? But Kirk knew firsthand about that. His own father hadn't believed in him. Thank God, he'd had his grandparents. But who did Bobby Joe have?

With fisted hands, Kirk barely restrained himself from not hitting the man. How could a man cut down his own flesh and blood, his own son, and slash his pride with a razor-sharp word? With his jaw clenched, he said in a measured tone, "The first d-d-day I went to Miss Montgomery's c-c-class—" he looked at Shannon, sitting prim and proper in her seat, her hands clasped tightly in her lap, her knuckles stark white "—I was a mite n-n-nervous. But Bobby Joe was there. He made me feel right at home."

The man's mouth fell open, and he sucked in a dribble of tobacco juice. "You were goin' to speech? Like Bobby Joe?"

"Y-y-yes, sir. Been having problems ever since I got my head kicked in last year by that b-b-bounty bull, Zorro."

Mr. Dooley's Adam's apple bobbed. He stared, silent as a fly stuck in a spider's web. Readjusting his baseball cap that Kirk recognized as the same kind Bobby Joe always wore, the man said, "You don't say."

Kirk nodded and grinned, no longer ashamed of his stutter, but now damn glad he had it. His gaze met his little friend's, who just wanted his daddy's unbridled love. "Bobby Joe's a good k-k-kid. He'd make a fine cowboy." Slowly he looked back at the father, feeling pity for a man who couldn't love his own son for who or what he was. "Think he could take on a buckin' bronc or even a r-r-rank bull in a few years."

Wanting to show his support to Bobby Joe, he took off his hat and set it on the little boy's head. The black Stetson practically swallowed the kid's face. Bobby Joe pushed it up and stared at Kirk. Surprise and confusion darkened his brown eyes to almost black.

"Watch this for me, okay?" Kirk asked.

Bobby Joe's eyes widened. In a whisper, he said, "Okay."

"When they play the 'Star S-S-Spangled Banner,' hold it against your chest."

Bobby Joe nodded.

"Isn't proper to wear a hat then. Gotta show respect for Old Glory." His gaze swerved to Shannon. She smiled at him, her encouraging smile. "And take care of Miss Montgomery for me, too," Kirk added.

Again the little boy nodded as Kirk turned away. He winked at Shannon then headed back toward the livestock. For the first time in the last year, he felt good about stuttering. Of course, he'd exaggerated it for Mr. Dooley's benefit. In fact, he'd actually enjoyed the surprised look on the man's face. The thick-headed dimwit didn't know a good thing when he had one. Bobby Joe was a smart kid, all he needed was a little encouragement, a little faith and belief in himself.

Kirk hoped he'd portrayed Bobby Joe in a whole new light for his dad. Maybe that in itself was the silver lining along the dark cloud of his accident and rehabilitation. That and meeting Shannon.

Thunder rumbled like a drumroll. The gray clouds overhead shifted uneasily, reminding Shannon of the cowboys she'd seen with the livestock: nervous, jumpy, on edge. She stood in the stands with the rest of the crowd, and her gaze flicked toward Bobby Joe. He held Kirk's black hat against his small chest. From the loudspeakers, the national anthem burst into the arena. Bobby Joe glanced up at his dad, elbowed him and pointed to his cap. Mr. Dooley frowned and slowly removed his cap and placed it over his heart.

Smiling to herself, she thought Bobby Joe might start making improvements. After her talk with his mother last week, she'd learned that his parents were separated. The problem seemed to be his dad's intolerance and gruff attitude.

She stared out at the cowboys and cowgirls on horseback, lined up along the rails of the arena. In the center two riders waved the American and Texas flags. Just to their left Kirk settled a white straw hat that looked like it belonged to Trey on his head. As the final notes of the "Star Spangled Banner" echoed through the arena, Kirk spurred Ginger into a slow walk behind the flag bearers.

Shannon admired his broad shoulders, his straight back that bent and swayed in accord with Ginger's steps, and his long, powerful legs, encased in rawhide leather chaps. As he rounded the final turn before leaving the arena, he tipped his hat and winked at her. Her heart swelled with pride. Not only because of his handsome good looks, which she'd noticed other women admiring, but also because of the way he'd handled Bobby Joe's father.

Earlier she'd seen the tick of anger in Kirk's jaw and his tightly fisted hands. But when he'd stood up for his little friend, even his debilitating stutter hadn't stopped him. He hadn't clammed up like he usually did when he felt ashamed at his stammering, but he'd spoken, halting though it was, like a proud, confident man.

He'd proven to Mr. Dooley that a man could be tough, a real man, even with a disability.

Looking back, she realized his stutter had been more pronounced than usual. Over the last few weeks, he'd made such progress. She couldn't believe he'd regressed now because of his anger at Bobby Joe's father. Had he done it on purpose? Knowing that when his words came from his heart, he usually spoke without hesitation, she realized he'd stuttered for Mr. Dooley's benefit.

She marveled at his care and concern for a child he barely knew. Deep in her heart she knew Kirk Mann was a good person. Someone she was proud of, someone she wanted to know better.

"Welcome, folks, to the Mesquite Championship Rodeo," the announcer said, interrupting her thoughts.

Tingling from the discovery of her own true feelings, she sat on the edge of the metal chair. She opened the front flap of the program Kirk had given her and skimmed the schedule of events as the announcer continued. Distant lightning brightened the sky like a dozen flickering fireflies among the heavy clouds.

"We got some lively action for you tonight. There's some pretty mean broncs here, who've got quite a kick and wiggle. They're gonna try and buck each and every cowboy off. But our men are fine athletes. They're gonna do their best for you. So give 'em a round of applause whether they take home a jingle in their pockets or a bootful of dirt."

The crowd cheered, whooping and hollering as if the Dallas Cowboys had again won the Super Bowl. Shannon smelled the tangy whiff of barbecue in the evening air and sipped her sweet, icy cola. New to this world of bulls and broncs, she absorbed the sights and sounds of horses bucking and the metal pens clanging like discordant bells as she waited for Kirk to return. Enthralled with an environment that seemed to fit him like his snug jeans, she wanted to know what the allure was for him, why he loved the rodeo, why he'd ridden bulls. Maybe watching the cowboys tonight, she could better understand the man she'd come to know and care for.

"We're gonna start this rowdy night off with a little calf ropin'," the announcer said. "It's the fastest man with horse and rope that's gonna win big tonight. Give a nice Texas welcome to our first cowboy. He's here all the way from Medicine Bow, Wyoming...."

Kirk sat next to her, and for a moment Shannon lost her concentration. Glad that he'd returned, she settled into her seat, relaxing now with him there.

"Do you want to go?" he asked.

"No. Let's stay." She glanced away from him, embarrassment heating her skin. Could he tell how she felt? How her feelings had changed toward him? "For a while."

"Are you sure?" His gaze probed hers.

She gave him a tentative smile. "Yes."

He reached down and plucked his hat off of Bobby Joe's head. "Thanks, cowboy." The little boy looked back with a grin. "And thanks for takin' care of my g-g-girl." He winked at Shannon.

Her insides heated, warming with the look in his gray eyes that resembled smoldering charcoal. *His* girl.

She liked the sound of that. She liked the thought of being with him. Not as student and teacher. Somehow, that didn't frighten her anymore.

"Bobby Joe did a very good job," she said.

Kirk clasped the boy's shoulder. "I knew he would. Are you having a good time with your d-d-dad?"

"Yep," Bobby Joe said. "I'm gonna be a cowboy, like you."

"You can do it." Kirk clasped Shannon's hand. The rough calluses along his palm and his stroking fingers ignited a heat inside her.

"How about you?" he asked her. "Are you having a good time?"

She nodded, unable to voice her emotions.

He squeezed her hand. "I'm glad you're here with me now."

His words wrapped around her like a silk ribbon, tying her insides into knots of desire. "Me, too."

He leaned toward her, his warm breath tingling her face with the scent of wintergreen, and pressed a gentle kiss to her forehead. "I think we've got something here. I don't ever want to lose you."

"I'm not going anywhere," she said, filled with conviction. Whether she understood his rodeo life or not, she knew it was a part of him, sewn into the fabric of his being in a tightly knit weave. What he'd done, what he'd survived, made him who he was today—a strong, proud cowboy.

In a whisper caress of a promise, he kissed her, his lips touching hers for the briefest of moments, but long enough to titillate her nerve endings. The air around them seemed electrified from the coming storm or their attraction, she didn't know which.

The rodeo events passed from one into another, from calf roping to bronc riding. Shannon barely noticed whether the cowboys scored big or landed face-down in the dirt. Only aware of Kirk, she noticed each time he shifted in his seat, stretched out his leg, rubbed his knee. He'd said once that the weather affected his old injuries. She wondered if he ached now with the approaching storm.

While cowgirls spurred their mounts around barrels, racing for the fastest times, Kirk explained the different events to her and patiently answered Bobby Joe's questions. When the bull riding started, she riveted her attention to that end of the arena, curious about the life Kirk had once led. As a bull rattled a chute, her body tensed, imagining what Kirk must have been like as a bull rider.

"Look at chute number one, folks," the announcer said, his voice sounded like a car backfiring. "That's Spike. A solid black Brangus with hook 'em horns. Watch out, cowboy! He's a live one!"

The chute sprang open, the bull lurched forward, and the cowboy sailed through the air and landed like a wet washcloth. The rodeo clowns raced in front of the bull, confusing him with their flapping arms and brightly colored outfits. The cowboy skittered like a crab out of the way, dusted himself off and left the arena with a scowl on his young face.

"Got whipped down," Kirk said with a shake of his head.

"What's that?" she asked, looking up the cowboy's name in the program.

"His timing was off." He took off his hat and rested one hand on the dented crown. "Gotta be moving forward when the bull jumps." He lifted his hat, his hand inching toward the front. He demonstrated with his hat the movements of the bull and rider. Bobby Joe turned around in his seat, absorbing every word Kirk muttered. "Otherwise you're too far back on the bull when he's at the peak of his jump. That's when he ducks his head and kicks his feet. If you're back too far, you're gonna go aerial."

Kirk shifted to the edge of his seat. "Watch this one. The bull's Tornado. Named 'cause he likes to spin." He settled his Stetson back on his head, and Bobby Joe swung around to watch. "Marty there's a good rider, but he's left-handed."

"And that's bad for a bull rider?" she asked, watching Kirk's eyes glitter like metal in the hot sun. Her stomach knotted.

"Not bad. Unless a bull likes to spin to the right. And this one does."

The chute clanged open and the bull shot into the arena. Tornado jumped once, the rider hanging on tight, but then the bull veered to his right, spinning in a tight circle. The cowboy made it halfway through the first spin then lost his balance. He hung on to the side of the bull. His body flapped like a broken doll then collapsed into the dirt.

Shannon clamped her hand over her mouth, covering a scream. The bullfighting clowns steered the bull away from Marty, and other cowboys rushed forward to carry the limp rider to safety.

"Is he all right?" she asked, her back stiff, her hand gripping Kirk's arm.

Kirk didn't answer, his gaze steady on the bent heads of cowboys sitting along the rail.

"Don't worry, folks," the announcer said. "Marty Cason's up and walking back there. Tornado must've knocked the wind out of him."

Kirk gave a knowing smile, one of both relief and empathy. "That can hurt," he said. "But he should be okay. If the bull spins toward your grip hand, then that makes it easier. But you got more forces pulling against you if the bull spins the opposite way. Like Tornado did."

Her body slowly thawed in the aftermath. She didn't know if she'd ever understand the brutality, the reasoning or the temptation to play with death. But she'd begun to understand that there was a philosophy to riding bulls, a strategy that Kirk seemed to know well. That comforted her somewhat. She'd thought bull riding entailed grabbing on and holding on with all your might for eight seconds. But she sensed there was more to this sport than she'd expected.

Looking at Kirk's profile, his sharp-edged nose, determined chin and scar slicing along his temple, she didn't know why he'd ever wanted to ride. What was the attraction? A moment of heart-stopping fear? The surge of adrenaline once he'd survived?

Confused, she sat in silence, not knowing how to react, feeling a storm escalate inside her. Like the

weighted clouds above the arena, dark and bloated
with rain, dread filled her with uncertainty. Kirk had
seemed concerned for his friend Marty, but then easily dismissed the accident with a casual line of logic.
To her it all seemed ludicrous, a daring stunt that
could land someone in a satin-lined coffin.

"Okay, folks," the announcer said, "you don't
want to miss this event. We've matched one heck of a
tough cowboy against one mean bull."

"Smiling Sam," Kirk said, his voice almost
drowned out by the announcer's explanation of a
bounty bull, "and Zorro." He looked at Shannon, his
eyes narrowed slits of steel. "This is the one."

"The one what?" She looked toward the number
four chute. A bull, dark as midnight, bucked against
the rider settling on his back. She recognized it as the
one Trey had attempted to ride, the one that had
charged Kirk. The metal gate rattled, the bells
wrapped around the bull's middle clanged. Her eyes
widened, and she knew.

Before Kirk spoke another word. Before the bull
exploded from the chute. This was the bull that had
almost killed her cowboy.

She'd tried to imagine the bull once, when Trey told
her of the bull who'd almost killed Kirk, but seeing the
real snorting, heaving mass of muscles gave weight to
her fears. She imagined the two-thousand-pound bull
stomping on Kirk, crushing his body, tearing the life
from his lungs. Her own chest tightened. What must
he be thinking at this moment? She remembered him

talking of his fear, his voice catching, his face reddening.

She focused on Kirk rather than on the ride about to take place and her own fears. With his hand tightly gripped in hers, she hoped to help him through this difficult time. His fingers seemed unresponsive, not curling around hers as they usually did. His muscles tensed, and his skin felt hot to the touch. She looked at him. He seemed preoccupied. It was like he'd changed before her very eyes, becoming a different man than the one she thought she'd understood a moment ago. His eyes narrowed to needle-sharp points.

"One month," he said to himself, his voice firm, his lips compressed in a thin line. "One month," he repeated in a whisper obviously meant for himself. And Zorro.

She heard the conviction in his voice, and it sent a cold slice of fear down her spine. "And what?" Her voice sounded hoarse, but he didn't seem to hear her. Tugging on his arm, she repeated the question. "What happens then?"

Slowly he looked at her, but without really seeing her. His focus seemed somewhere else. His eyes glinted with steely determination. "I've drawn Zorro. In a month I'll ride him. My last ride."

Blood drained from her face; her vision blurred, spinning her into a vortex of reeling emotions. Was he crazy? Didn't he understand he could die? Didn't he care?

Her breath caught on the lump in her throat as she realized that she'd made a heart-breaking mistake. She blinked back hot, stinging tears. The man she loved... Loved? Yes, loved. He cared more for a daredevil thrill than anything else...even life itself. Icy fear frosted the blood in Shannon's veins.

And that stopped her heart cold.

Chapter Eight

The brutal dance started. Beneath the canopy of rain-swollen clouds, copper bells clanked, creating a cacophony with the cheers from the crowd. To some it might seem blaring, a disjointed rhythm, but to Kirk it sounded better than a country-western band, a blend of sounds that underscored the action in the arena.

The rider and bull moved as one, a union of steel determination and bulging, straining muscles. Grit versus power. Sam Allen, his cowboy hat tipped low over his forehead, followed each of Zorro's twists, turns and jumps, countering with his own precise movements. Kirk could almost feel the impact on his own joints and bones as the bull's hooves crashed into the dirt, jarring the stubborn cowboy and trying to dislodge him from his precarious perch.

A tan cloud of dirt enveloped the pair, making the first four seconds seem like a slow-action film. Then Zorro stopped, his knees locked. His broad sides heaved. He snorted and tossed a look over his shoulder, his eyes wild and rolling.

The crowd yelled, encouraging bull and rider to finish the duel. Lightning flashed overhead, a flicker of white light against the starless sky. The mere second seemed frozen, like suspended animation.

Kirk held his breath. He knew Sam would receive points for both his and the bull's performances. And Kirk knew better than anyone how unpredictable Zorro could be. Sweat dribbled down his spine, a cold shiver ripped through him.

Spur him, Kirk thought as his hands clenched. A cowboy often had to goad a cranky bull into a better show. He watched Sam do the only thing he could do to salvage his ride. The desperate rider dug his spurs into the bull's flanks.

In an explosion of muscle, anger and power, Zorro jumped. All four hooves kicked off the ground. His broad back arched. His shoulders bulged. His back legs sliced through the air like blunted knives.

Sam slid too far back on Zorro, off center and out of sync. The dance had ended almost before it had begun. In a last-ditch effort, Sam jerked his free arm back, trying to throw himself forward, to regain his balance.

But the bull had won.

Zorro whirled to the left, turning like a corkscrew, away from Sam's grip hand. This time, losing his center, the rider tilted backward and fell sideways. His body jerked off the bull, but his hand hung in the grip. Sam flailed, his boots raking across the dirt.

Kirk jerked upright in reflex. He knew the searing pain. He felt it now for his friend. He remembered the panic, the inability to protect himself from a charging steam engine, the bitter taste of dirt, the acrid smell of his own fear. Hang on for a ride through hell, he thought, clenching his fists, wanting to help his friend.

The Brahma leapt and turned, jumped and twirled in a tighter circle, forcing Sam beneath him. Zorro's front legs crashed down on Sam, bending the cowboy like a twig beneath a full ton, breaking bones, ripping flesh.

A gasp of horror echoed around him. Kirk stood, his body tense, wanting to leap into the arena to help his friend. The bullfighters moved in, trying to detour the bull. Sam tumbled beneath stomping, angry hooves. He curled his body into a ball, a bloody, crippled mass, and tried to cover his head with his arm. His gloved grip hand flopped at an awkward angle.

Oh God, not again! Kirk's temple throbbed with memories. Sweat broke out on his forehead. Like every other cowboy in the stands or on the gates around the arena, he felt helpless, unable to help a friend, unable to prevent a bloody wreck.

Those around him had joined Kirk on their feet. The tense silence stretched like a taut calving rope, the announcer floundered for words. The moment seemed to last forever, and yet Kirk knew it only took seconds. But, God, the damage done in a few short seconds could end a man's career... or his life.

Without thinking, just gut instinct acting, he bounded down the concrete stairs and gripped the rail. He gauged the drop—at least twenty feet. Frustrated, he was relegated to the sidelines to watch other cowboys who were closer to the action flood from the rails and try to save Sam.

Zorro ducked his head, butting the downed cowboy with his horns. Untamed hooves crashed down on Sam's limp body.

The clowns waved and hollered. They threw their own bodies in the bull's line of sight. Cowboys skittered about the bull like ants trying to stop a bulldozer. Zorro veered, charging one of the clowns, but slammed into a painted barrel, knocking it and rolling it over and over.

Sam lay in the dirt, unmoving, bent as a gnarled tree limb. Cowboys rushed toward him as the clowns managed to usher Zorro out of the arena.

Fear turned Kirk's blood ice-cold, freezing him in his spot. It looked bad, damn bad.

Down in the arena Trey dropped to his knees beside their friend. Kirk's brother leaned way over Sam as other cowboys crowded in close. Then abruptly Trey sat back on his heels, visibly pale and shaken. Sam didn't move. But Trey waved toward the paramedics and said something to Sam.

Something that Trey had probably said to Kirk when he'd had his wreck almost a year ago. Something inane, yet at the same time, something that gave the wounded cowboy something to grasp besides the pain, the blinding, all-consuming pain. To Kirk, Trey's voice had been a lifeline, pulling him from the murky blackness of unconsciousness.

At the time Kirk had wanted to drown in the red swirling pain, lose himself in the darkness, forget everything...die. But Trey's voice had called him back. When he'd come to, the pain had been horrendous. But the voice had saved him, saved him from oblivion, saved him from death.

He knew that now.

The drone of the announcer, trying to ease the crowd's concerns, reverberated off the steel benches and prodded Kirk into action. His heart pumped hard and fast, frantic and fearful. His ears roared with the sound of rushing blood. He strode toward the nearest exit, brushing past anyone who got in his way. Not that he could help, but he had to be there. Just in case.

A quick tug on his arm made him glance back. Shannon.

She opened her mouth to speak, but no words came. Fear etched her hazel eyes. Concern wrinkled her brow and compressed her lips into a thin line. She looked scared; bone-chillingly scared.

Finally she said, "I'm coming with you."

He nodded, grabbed her hand and led her at a fast clip down the walkway toward the chutes. He felt better with her near him. Still, a cold knot formed in his stomach. For the first time he thought objectively about his own wreck. What had his family and friends, especially Trey, felt when he'd been stomped on by Zorro?

The sound of his boot heels thwacking the concrete walk echoed in his head, a harsh cadence that emphasized the fear building inside him. He knew the ambulance was waiting for Sam, the paramedics probably already working on him.

As if his own accident had just happened, he could almost hear Trey's voice calling to him, like he had a year ago. Distant and calm, his brother had said, "Kirk? You hear me?" He'd felt his brother's hand squeeze his arm. Pain stabbed him, but he'd prayed for it to remain. That way he knew he still lived, for the moment, anyway. "You're gonna be okay." Trey's voice had lent Kirk strength. "You're gonna be okay!"

Then he'd floated on a soft, white cloud, hearing only the beat of his own heart and the sound of his breathing, seeing only a pale light around him, encasing him in a powerful warmth. When he'd woken three days later, his brother had been by his side, Trey's eyes red and shadowed with smudges of exhaustion.

Kirk hoped that someone, maybe Trey, was now giving Sam the contact he needed, a lifeline through the red fog of pain.

The silence sounded ominous as he walked down the long row of metal chutes. Hay, manure and horse sweat blended into a fierce odor. The lights of the ambulance flashed red and blue, slashing at the darkness in the parking lot. At the end of the runway, he saw Trey and other cowboys, their heads bent, arms crossed, faces solemn. The gurney sat at the back of the ambulance, the doors wide, the paramedics jabbing needles into Sam.

"Sam!" A piercing cry cut through the fearful silence. "Sam!" Geena, his wife, ran toward the ambulance, her pregnant frame awkward and ungainly.

Trey stepped in front of her, his hands grasping her shoulders. He blocked her view with his wide shoulders.

"Let go of me!" Geena pushed, slapped, shoved against him.

He hauled her against his chest, imprisoning her arms with his. His head bent toward her, and Kirk saw his lips move in a whispered plea. His embrace gentled then, his hands clasping her to him. His body accommodated her round, bloated belly that stretched her floral romper tight across her middle. She bucked once, twice, then she sagged against Trey, dry sobs racking her body.

Her cries filled the walkway, tearing through Kirk, ripping open his heart and showing him what he hadn't seen last year when he'd been in Sam's position.

And it gave him a glimpse into the future.

This is what Shannon would go through if he had another wreck. He squeezed his eyes shut, blocking the image, refusing to acknowledge the possibility. As a rule he'd never looked at death, until his accident had forced a closer examination. He'd realized then that life was short. Shorter for some than others. And he'd rearranged his priorities. He'd changed.

The siren wailed. Jarred back to the present, Kirk opened his eyes and watched the ambulance pull out, a slow procession around the parked cars toward the highway. He whispered a prayer for Sam ... for Geena ... and for their unborn child.

Several women, wives of other riders and barrel racers, women who knew the brutal facts about life on the rodeo circuit, surrounded Geena. Their arms offered comfort. Their tears expressed their empathy, their own fears. Their whispered words prayed for heavenly guidance. Together they led her away. Someone, probably all of them, would take her to the hospital.

His throat tight, Kirk walked up to his brother and touched his dampened, tear-streaked shoulder. Startled, Trey's muscles jerked, and he looked up, his eyes red rimmed, his mouth drawn tight as a bowstring. Kirk couldn't voice the question that he somehow already knew the answer to.

"How is he?" Shannon's voice sounded loud in the stillness, but he knew she'd whispered the question. Her arms were wrapped around her shivering frame.

Trey looked from Shannon to Kirk, then shook his head.

"Damn." Kirk turned away, unable to grasp the meaning, unable to think of Smiling Sam Allen dead. His chest contracted, squeezing the breath out of him. It should have been a reality of his profession, but somehow cowboys never contemplated the consequences. He, like all the rest, lived for the moment. No regrets, no *what ifs*. Kirk knew that men who lived on the edge often fell, sometimes died. But knowing the facts didn't make the reality any easier to accept.

He thought of Sam, his wife, their unborn child. It could have been Kirk a year ago. A misplaced horn or hoof, and he himself would have taken a trip to the morgue. It would have been better that way, he thought, since he'd had no obligations. Not like Sam who had a pregnant wife and more responsibilities.

Still holding Shannon's hand, he squeezed and pulled her against him. She felt stiff, cold. He enfolded her in his arms, trying to warm the chill that had seeped into him. Now, he thanked God that it hadn't been his time a year ago. Because now he had Shannon. And he needed her. He had a future planned with her in it, and he wanted to see his dreams fulfilled.

He knew it was selfish, and guilt inched its way through him, clawing at him with regret. But he couldn't look back now. He had to look forward.

Over the top of Shannon's head, he looked at Trey. "What about Geena?"

"I told her." Trey's voice cracked.

Kirk's throat convulsed.

"God, I had to tell her." Trey's eyes filled with unshed tears. He swallowed, his Adam's apple recoiling in his throat. "I promised . . . Sam . . ." He ducked his head and dug the toe of his boot into the dirt. "I said I'd help her out. You know, with the baby comin' and all."

Kirk nodded. It was a code with cowboys. They helped each other like family. They always had, and they always would. "We'll all help."

"I know." The bitter confusion in Trey's blue eyes chilled Kirk. "Why Sam?"

"I don't know," Kirk answered, expressing the same disbelief in the shake of his head. "I don't know."

Shannon pushed away from him, fire in her eyes turning the irises to golden flames. "It happened," she said, her voice a low hiss, "because he was foolish enough to get on the back of a dangerous bull. He took a risk." She blinked several times; tears dampened her dark lashes. Then she stared up at Kirk, a hard glint in her eyes, or maybe one of regret. "Like you've done before. Like you want to do again. A stupid, careless, foolish risk."

She turned on her heel and walked away from Kirk.

With each step her determination grew. Her footsteps quickened until she was running toward the parking lot. Shannon ran from Kirk, from his need to ride that damn bull and from her love for a man who took chances. Chances that were idiotic and dangerous. Chances that could cost him his life.

And her heart.

She'd been foolish to fall for a daredevil. She should have known better. Why hadn't she guarded her heart? Why had she fallen in love with Kirk? Love? Yes, the heart-wrenching pain in her chest told her it was love. But why?

Because, she told herself as she ran out into the parking lot, sprinkles of rain dotting her face, she couldn't help it. Falling in love with Kirk had been as easy as eating a batch of warm cookies. But now she regretted her carelessness. She'd been a fool. Heartache was her only reward. She'd pay the price. Again. In tears.

But not in tears at a funeral. She wouldn't be around if Kirk wanted to risk his neck.

Her heart pounded in her chest. Her lungs burned. Tears stung her eyes, searing a path down her cheeks. Why, oh why, couldn't he be a normal man? Why couldn't he run his ranch and give up this crazy notion? Why couldn't he be content to just love her?

Thunder roared like an angry animal. Lightning flashed like fangs—a jagged crack of white tore open the black sky just the way her heart had been ripped in two. She wanted to shout into the night where no one could hear her. Wail her despair, cry for her own loss.

She stopped, her knees locked and her hands clenched at her sides. Her breath came in gasps, shuddering through her. She looked up at the dark threatening clouds, heavy with rain.

"Why?" she cried to the heavens. Why had she fallen in love with Kirk?

A ragged sob wrenched free, and she covered her mouth with her hand, unwilling to release her tears for a mistake she'd been stupid enough to make for the second time in her life. Somehow she knew that tears could never cleanse the hurt and anguish. Nothing would. Time might ease the heartache, but she'd always carry the scars of a love that should never have been.

And now what?

The rain started, a slow, steady shower, growing heavier with each minute, soaking her shirt and molding it to her breasts. A muddy puddle formed around her boots.

The empty, forsaken cars surrounding her reflected the bitter loneliness she felt so acutely. She stood in the rain without a car, without a way home. Rain battered the hoods of trucks, a hollow sound that resembled the void in her soul. A blackness that seemed to swallow her. She felt lost, alone. Nowhere to go. No way to get there. No one to go with.

The sounds of the rodeo drifted toward her: the announcer's voice, and the crowd heading toward shelter by the concessions. Nothing had changed for anyone. Life went on. Except for a cowboy, his wife and an unborn child. Sam Allen was dead. Now his wife would have to continue without him.

And Shannon felt as if her life had been sucked into a vacuum; suddenly she was locked into a lifetime of solitude. She knew it was over between Kirk and her. She couldn't watch him kill himself like Sam. Like Evan. She wouldn't. She'd never survive that.

She'd rather think of him alive, without her, than dead.

The splash of boots in mud puddles startled her, creating a sucking sound with each step as the muck and mud pulled against the soles. Wary, and well aware that she was a lone woman in a deserted parking lot, Shannon whirled around. Kirk walked toward her, his face dark and grim, his hands clenched, rainwater dripping from the brim of his hat.

"Leave me alone," she said, turning away but not knowing where to go.

He ignored her demand and walked right up to her, grabbed her shoulders and spun her around. He hauled her against his broad chest. His eyes looked like cold, hard steel, boring into her. "I lost a f-f-friend tonight. I don't want to lose you. I need you."

She pushed away from his chest. "No, you don't. Don't you see? You need this." She jerked her chin toward the arena. "The rodeo. You need the thrill of the moment. You need the excitement. You need to risk your life."

His jaw flexed. "I have to ride. Just once more. That's all." His eyes softened. "Then I'll retire."

"But what next?" she asked.

"What do you mean?"

"I mean, what next? You'll miss the adrenaline rush. What'll you do? Drive like a maniac down the road..."

"Th-th-th—" He stopped and ground his teeth in frustration. Humiliation clouded his eyes.

Her heart softened, and she placed a comforting hand over his heart.

He squeezed his eyes shut and took a ragged breath. "Th-that's what this is all about?" His eyes opened and gazed at her with a hopeless need. "Evan."

The name hung between them like a challenge, a threat. She realized then that Evan had always come between them. Not because of an overwhelming love for her dead boyfriend, but fear that it would be like that again. She knew that in most ways Kirk was not like Evan, but that in his core, the very essence of his nature, he was. He was a daredevil. That would never change. And Evan would haunt them forever.

"Yes," she said. "Evan." Her fingers dug into his shirt, not wanting to let Kirk go, but knowing there was no other way. "I won't go to another funeral."

"Damn." His hands squeezed her upper arms, biting into her soft flesh. She winced, and he immediately released her. "Are you all right?"

"Yes." She rubbed her arms, keeping them crossed over her chest for protection. Not from Kirk, but from herself. Because she knew that if she felt even a moment of hope, she'd rush back into his arms. For there she felt secure.

"I'm not Evan." His voice sounded strong and sure, then softened to barely a whisper. "I won't hurt you."

"You already have."

He flinched as if she'd slapped him, and she regretted her harsh words. His eyes darkened, and he took a step forward then stopped. He reached for her, but she backed away. His hand slowly fell to his side. "How?"

She knew he wasn't at fault. He couldn't deny who he was, what he wanted. But he had to know the truth. "By wanting to ride Zorro again."

He sighed, lifted his Stetson and plowed his fingers through his hair. Raindrops splattered against his face. "Can't you understand? Just once. H-h-help me through this." His voice cracked. "I need you."

"No." Her heart contracted with acute pain. "I can't."

"You mean you won't."

Tears burning her eyes, she said, "Yes."

"Don't you understand I'm not like Evan? Th-th-this," he said, glancing over his shoulder at the lighted arena, "is different. I don't want to take the risks that I used to." He took another step forward, closing in on her before she could back away.

"I want a future." His eyes misted. "I want you in my life." In a whisper-soft caress, he stroked her cheek.

The words she'd wanted to hear from him sounded empty, without promise. Her whole being cried out for him, but she held firm, her arms still clasped across her middle.

"But this...Zorro...is something I have to face. Once more."

She grasped his wrist, holding his hand against her neck. Her pulse throbbed in her breast. "Why?"

His thumb slid down the column of her throat. He stared at her mouth for a long moment. Her body responded. She wanted his kiss, but she couldn't...wouldn't succumb. The attraction was strong, more powerful than anything she'd ever known, but the problem between them could never be solved.

"Tell me why," she said, desperate to understand why it was all ending before it had really begun.

In a soft tone he said, "Because I have to face my fear."

"Why?" Her vision blurred with tears. "That bull just killed your friend! Why can't you just live with it?"

"Like you do? L-l-lock up my heart and throw away the k-k-key so that nothing or no one can ever hurt me? That's fine, as long as you don't ever want to live or be loved."

"Love hurts."

He wiped away the tears and raindrops wetting her cheeks. "It doesn't have to." He pulled her against him, shielding her with his body from the rain. "Let me show you."

She stayed there almost too long. Her hands moved to encircle his waist, then she caught herself. Shaking her head, she stepped out of his embrace.

He let her go, but he didn't stop trying to persuade her. "Shannon, don't you see that you're running from your fear? Face it. I'll help you. C-c-come to me. Stand by me through this, and I'll help you through yours. Then we can walk away t-t-together, hand in hand. Always."

"No." She took another step back. "I can't." Her voice was almost lost in the rumble of thunder overhead, but the look on his face told her he'd heard clearly enough.

"Why?" he asked, a catch in his voice.

"Because you have a death wish."

He laughed, a caustic sound. "Is that what you think?"

She nodded, tears choking her.

"Maybe I did once. I don't know. All that changed a year ago. I saw that tonight. Now I want to live. I want to love you."

She wanted to open to him, and her arms longed to embrace him. She ached for him, his touch, his kiss. But she steeled herself. It would never work. Never. At least, not while he still had a crazy need.

"But..." She let the word hang, hoping that he'd say there was nothing standing between them.

He nodded slowly, a grim determination in his eyes. "*But* I have to ride Zorro. I have to deal with my fear. Once and for all."

"That's your pride talking." A spark of anger ignited and with it hope. Maybe he would walk away. Maybe he'd give up this crazy notion. For her. Maybe if he loved her enough...

"Yeah, it probably is."

"Then don't." She moved forward and grabbed his hand. She held it against her breast, letting him feel the frantic beat of her heart. "Please. For me." Her throat burned, and tears stung her eyes. "Just walk away now. With me. Forget this. Forget Zorro. You don't have to prove anything. I know you're a man. And that's enough for me."

"I have to p-p-prove it to myself." He tapped his chest. "*I* don't know that. I can't let fear have the last word."

"If you die, then it will." She knew she sounded petulant, like a spoiled child, but she couldn't stop herself. She felt desperate, clawing at every last chance. "If you love me, you could walk away."

He shook his head. "That's not how it works, Shannon. You're hiding behind a wall of fear. I don't see you trying to beat it. The fear's winning. M-m-meet me halfway. Together we'll get through this. Then we can go on. We'll be stronger."

She let go of his hand, and the hope that had surged within her died. He wouldn't change. He couldn't. His stubborn cowboy pride would make him take this foolish risk. If so, he'd do it without her.

With a last sniff, she swiped at the tears on her face. "We're at a stalemate. It just won't work. You won't compromise, and I can't."

He stared at her for a long moment. "Then that's it?"

She nodded, pressing her lips inward to keep them from quivering.

"You can just walk away? Forget?"

She averted her gaze, unable to look at the disappointment in his somber gray eyes, the deep sadness.

"You say that *I'm* selfish in th-th-this, but it's you, too."

Stunned, she looked back at him.

He shook his head, his shoulders slumping with defeat. Rubbing his jaw, he gazed up at the slackening rain. Water dripped from his chin and rolled off the back of his hat. He took several deep breaths, then said, "Come on, I'll take you home."

Chapter Nine

It was time. No more stalling, no backing out. Time to pay the devil his due. Kirk poised himself over the heaving mass of muscles. The mottled red and brown Brahma stomped on the weathered floorboards, his hooves scraping the splintered wood.

Perspiration trickled along Kirk's hairline. At a rodeo in a Podunk little town west of Dallas, he was about to make his much-anticipated comeback. It mattered little to him if he made money today or not. What mattered was that this would help prepare him to meet Zorro again in two weeks. Face-to-face, grit pitted against rawhide muscle.

Clapping his hat down on his head, Kirk wrapped the leather grip around his right hand and pulled it tight. He lowered himself onto the back of the ugly son-of-a-gun bull by the name of Sunrise, Sunset, and clutched the bull's bulging sides with his thighs.

The Brahma lurched forward and butted his head against the railing. The bells clanked, and the chute groaned. Kirk steadied himself, his left hand locked on the side rail, then he glanced up at Trey.

"You ready?" His brother leaned over the side of the chute.

Kirk nodded, then focused his attention between the bull's yellowish horns. He was ready. Ready for anything.

He felt nothing. No fear. No excitement. A blessed nothing masked the fear that had once consumed him. Now, he held on to his gritty determination. Nothing mattered but this. This moment. This confrontation with himself, more than the bull.

With two quick nods, he signaled Trey to release the gate. It creaked. Hooves clamoring, the bull lunged for freedom.

Maybe it had been too long since he'd felt the raw power of a bull bucking beneath him. Maybe he'd lost what little talent he'd had. Whatever the reason, Kirk had no time to think, only to react.

In the span of two seconds Sunrise, Sunset leapt straight into the air, then dropped hard and fast. Kirk's bones grated against his joints. He clenched his teeth and squeezed the handhold.

The riotous, jolting movements pushed Kirk too far back on the bull. He lost his balance and his seating.

One final thrusting buck later and Kirk flew up, then slammed down on the packed dirt of the arena, down and out. He glanced over his shoulder, saw the clowns head off the bull, then slowly rose to his feet. His bad knee buckled, but he caught himself, hobbled once then righted himself.

Disgusted at his performance, he bent down for his hat and slapped it against the back of his jeans. Dust ballooned around him. Damn, he thought, he'd have to do better to stay on Zorro... to stay alive.

He clenched his jaw against the pain in his knee. The old injury protested, questioning Kirk's sanity. Stiffening his walk, he tried to hide his limp. The conciliatory applause of the crowd rang in his ears, and he cursed himself.

Climbing the nearest rail, he ignored the stares of the other cowboys. He needed a moment alone. With agitated steps he walked down the corridor past the angry bulls, toward the green bucking broncs. Passing a stall, he yanked a blade of hay out of a fresh bale and stuck it between his teeth.

The sweet taste emphasized the acrid bite of defeat. Rolling the thin reed across his tongue, he shifted the dry stalk to the other side of his mouth. He leaned against a roughened oak post and clapped his Stetson down low on his sweaty brow.

The sun felt hot, even though it rode low on the horizon, moseying the long, lonely day toward a longer, lonelier night. The back of his shirt, damp with sweat, clung to him. Dirt caked the back of his jeans and boots—evidence of his failure.

"How ya doin'?"

Kirk turned toward Trey and shrugged.

"Didn't ring your bell or nothin', did he?" His brother's brow crinkled with concern.

"Nope." He watched the next bull rider triumph, making the full eight seconds and racking up eighty-three points. "D-d-damn." He clenched his jaw, gritting his teeth and worrying about his stammer again. It crept back into his speech, like his fear stole its way into his soul.

"Hey," Trey clapped his hand on Kirk's shoulder and gave him a playful shake, "don't take it so hard. It'll take you a few weeks to get back in the saddle again."

Kirk nodded, knowing his brother was right. He should look at this ride positively. At least he'd mounted, ignored any residual fear and tried his luck. But he felt nothing now, nothing since he'd watched Shannon enter her apartment two weeks ago and close the door softly behind her, shutting him out. At that moment a weight had formed in his gut that he couldn't explain, couldn't get rid of. He'd turned off all emotions, not wanting to feel the pain or think about his loss.

Separated from Shannon, he'd managed to fill his days doing chores around the ranch and training himself for his return to the rodeo circuit. But the nights had been hell. Filled with visions of her, her sweet smile and comforting touch.

Then her words had come back to him, punched him in the gut with the same impact. "You have a death wish."

He wondered if she was right. Maybe he longed for death. An end. Maybe all bull riders did. Then he'd replay the gruesome event at the rodeo, reliving Sam's death, feeling the impact of each blow in his own gut.

His friend's death filled him with a deep sorrow that felt like a dark cloud surrounding him. He'd gone to Sam's funeral and to pay his respects to his friend's pregnant widow. It all left Kirk restless and confused.

If Shannon was right and he had a death wish, then life no longer mattered. He'd lost any reason to live when she'd closed her heart to him. Night after night he'd tossed and turned until the gray hours before dawn, then he'd risen with tired eyes, hoping he would work himself hard enough to induce a deep, exhausted sleep that night.

Propping his hip on a barrel, he felt the effects of his ride sinking into his tense shoulders, tight neck and sore butt. All just a part of his profession. Honestly, he thought, he should be glad he hadn't gotten his head busted in, with the way he'd ridden. Now he would do what he had to do. Prepare himself, make himself harder and stronger, in order to ride Zorro.

It was all he had left.

Shannon pushed the stubborn vacuum cleaner over her thick carpet, matching wills with her own determination. The humming roar deafened her to the tiny voice inside her head that berated her for her own foolishness. She wanted no lectures, even from herself, only the ability to go on with her life.

Trading the vacuum for a mop, she slapped the linoleum and pushed water around her kitchen, feeling about as strong as the limp cotton strands. She'd told Kirk exactly how she'd felt, frightened for his life, terrified of losing her own if he died. But each day since, she'd vacillated, swishing about like the sudsy water in her plastic bucket. One minute she felt strong enough to withstand her feelings, the next she succumbed to tears, wanting . . . needing Kirk back in her life.

Over the past three weeks, she'd realized she had never let go of Evan, never let go of her anger. The love had long since vanished, probably because it had only been infatuation, her need feeding his greed. But over the years she'd clung to the grief and anger like dust on window blinds. Now she needed something strong to wipe away the dirty residue that saturated her soul, to wash away the bitterness.

Her fear blocked out her love for Kirk, destroying the beauty of what could have been. Because she knew that Kirk, in all his strength and gentleness, could erase the pain. If she let him.

She cinched the trash bag and carted it outside onto the porch. The stillness of the hot night closed in upon her, suffocating her with the heat, forcing her back inside to the cool of her air conditioner.

Finished with her chores, she paced around her living room, tilting a picture then straightening a book on the shelf. Everything should have fallen into perfect alignment. But it hadn't. Her life seemed off balance, out of sync. And she knew why.

Kirk.

He'd made her life fun, enjoyable, relaxing. At the same time he'd invited her to share in the rich seasonings that life could offer. He'd shown her a new side to herself, a side she'd hidden from view for too long. But now the reflection of vulnerability stared back at her as she flicked a dust particle off the mirror in the entryway. The deep sadness transformed her eyes to pools of sorrow. Her face looked almost gaunt now, her cheeks thin.

He'd said it was her. Her selfishness that stood in their way. But was it her? Or was it Kirk's stubborn pride?

She sniffed back the hot tears. Not today. She didn't want to cry today. But she knew she would. When she finally sat down, or when she crawled into bed, before she drifted into a restless sleep, her walls would crumble and she'd think of him. The tears would well, and she'd be unable to stop them.

But not right now.

With his memory threatening her, she grabbed her feather duster and began to dust her apartment again, this time with determination that she would erase his memory. She'd let go of Kirk and go on with her life.

Suddenly she sat on her chintz-covered couch. The truth struck her. She buried her face in her hands. Tears ran through her fingers, hot and angry. With a true glimpse of herself, she realized she'd been at fault . . . not Evan . . . not even Kirk. She'd determined the course of her life. And she had control over the future. But that future was vacant without Kirk.

* * *

It felt tight, slim-fitting-jeans tight. The leather cords, woven close together, formed Kirk's grip, molding to the contours of his hand.

Most folks thought bull riders just held on for a helluva ride, but Kirk knew the ins and outs of his profession. Bull riding took a combination of gritty determination, stubborn pride, rehearsed skills, some talent and solid equipment. It was a rare cowboy who had the guts to challenge a raging bull, and a tenacious breed of man to survive.

Once more Kirk unwrapped and relooped the rigging around his grip hand, confident that it fit snug, confident that this was his night to ride.

In the small East Texas arena, the air weighed heavily, hot and damp, with the strong scent of pine. The town had a name that resembled many small towns across the country. Named for a bigger, more spectacular city, it offered only a red flashing light rather than a glittering skyline, and feed barns instead of department stores. A nothing town, on a nothing highway, with no particular distinction except it had a well-regarded rodeo every third weekend in May.

This ride tonight would finish his preparation for Zorro. Kirk felt ready, confident, focused. His body felt strong, wholly recovered, and his mind concentrated on his task. He palmed the top of his Stetson, lowering it to just above his eyebrows. With a final glance at the solid brown Brangus who pawed his cage with pent-up frustration, Kirk climbed the rails.

Careful to lower himself slowly onto the back of the bull, his spurs jingled as he balanced on the top bar. "Easy, b-b-boy. Easy."

"You got a mean one there," Trey said from behind him. "Radical's likely to turn on you."

Kirk nodded. "I'll be ready."

"I rode him over in Fort Worth last year."

"I remember." Kirk settled onto the bull and wrapped his hand with the leather rigging. "Got your b-b-butt kicked."

"Damn straight." Trey laughed. "He likes to charge left out of the chute. Hold tight, 'cause then he's got a high leap with a front-end drop."

With another nod, Kirk acknowledged Trey's repeated advice, then he rocked forward and back, finding the perfect spot on the bull's broad back. He absorbed the raw scent of sweat and fresh manure, the feel of muscle and sinew under him, the sight of Radical's bulging shoulders and crooked horns. This was it. He was ready. Now.

He gave the two standard nods. "Okay, okay."

The gate clanged open, and the bull lunged through the opening, ducking left. Kirk followed the bull's lead, countering his every move. Just as Trey had said, Radical leapt high, then his front legs and shoulders made a fast drop, jarring Kirk. But he held on, his knees clutching the bull, his body in the perfect position, reacting automatically to each move, each buck, each spin.

In a world known only to cowboys, Kirk heard only his heartbeat. He kept his eyes trained on the bull's head. Each second ticked by like a thousand. Still, Kirk danced with the bull who led him around one end of the arena in a quick three-step shuffle, rocking, dipping, twirling.

When the eight-second buzzer sounded, Kirk took his leave. He disengaged his grip hand and leapt clear of the bull. His feet landed, his good knee braced him, his bad knee caught. But he stood. With a quick glance over his shoulder, he watched the clowns distract the bull and maneuver the two thousand pounds of steely muscle out of the arena.

Then Kirk heard the roar of the crowd, the rumble of feet stomping the stands, the thunder of hands clapping. His fists clenched with exaltation. He'd done it. What he'd worked for, what he'd aimed for, what he'd needed.

"That's one heck of a cowboy, folks," the announcer said, his voice booming out of the speakers. "With a score of eighty-seven points, that puts him on top." The sound system crackled. "He's our winner this evening. Way to go, Kirk. Welcome back to the rodeo circuit."

He tipped his Stetson to the crowd and walked toward the nearest railing. His knee ached, the same old grinding pain that he'd grown accustomed to. He saw his friends, fellow cowboys and his brother, smiling and shouting congratulations on his winning score.

An automatic grin broke across his face, but the surge of excitement that he'd always experienced with each of his successes never came. His footsteps seemed wooden. His smile felt stiff. The cheers and congratulations sounded distant.

What was wrong with him? He'd worked hard for this, overcome a mountain of obstacles to get back to this. This should be a triumphant moment. The crowd seemed to think it was. And if that didn't convince him, Trey's beaming face should.

He thought of his life on the road, traveling from rodeo to rodeo, town to town, from one win to the next. He realized he'd once loved the thrill, the excitement, the challenge. But he'd changed. Not because of the accident. But because of Shannon.

An emptiness overwhelmed him. The victory felt hollow.

"That's wonderful, Bobby Joe! You're talking so much better." Shannon pressed a happy-face sticker that smelled like licorice to his shirt.

He smiled. The timidness had faded over the past few weeks, marking only part of his improvement. "Can I have a pief—" He ducked his head and tried again, forming the word slowly. "Pies-s-se of candy?"

"You sure can." She held out the fishbowl, full of brightly colored candies. "What do you say?"

"F-f-f—" He shook his head. "Thuh-ank you."

"Good." She smiled at him, pleased that he'd begun correcting his lisp. Although he still struggled, the wrong sounds usually popping out first, now he stopped himself and corrected his mistake, often overemphasizing and dragging out the correct sound.

It was a wonderful start. "I'm so proud of you, Bobby Joe."

He smiled, his cheeks dimpling.

She glanced at the clock on the wall. "It's time for you to go back to class. I'll see you on Monday, okay?"

"Okay." He stood and grabbed his cap and book.

"Are you going to see your daddy this weekend?" she asked.

"He'f— He's-s-s gonna take me to the rodeo tonight."

Shannon swallowed a sudden lump in her throat. She didn't want to think of rodeos and cowboys, of bulls and death. Because then she'd think of Kirk. "That's good." Struggling for control of her wavering voice, she reached for a stack of awards then changed the subject. "How would you like to show your daddy how well you've been doing in speech?"

Bobby Joe's eyes brightened, and he nodded.

"This says," she said as she filled in the blank spaces on the award, "that you've made a lot of progress in the last week." She held up the whale-shaped paper. "Can you read it for me?"

He studied the letters before reading in a halting manner. "Bobby Joe Dooley's done a whale of a good job."

He glanced back at her, checking to see if he'd read it correctly.

"Very good," she said. "You're reading wonderfully."

"I got a B this week," he said beaming.

"That's great!"

"I'm gonna take my report card for Kirk to fee ...
s-s-see tonight."

A dull ache throbbed in her breast at the sound of
his name. She couldn't help asking, "You're going to
see him ... at the rodeo?"

He nodded as he walked across the room, his cap set
crookedly on his head and his favorite Dr. Seuss book
tucked under his arm. He pulled open the door.
"Kirk's gonna ride that big, ugly bull. S-s-see ya
Monday."

Zorro. She knew. Her heart beat wildly, hammering fear through her veins. Why did Kirk have to ride?
What did he have to prove? All his awards should have
proven to him his ability.

Over the past few weeks, she'd questioned his mo-
tives, still not understanding, still groping for a reason. Did his pride ride solely on whether he could best
a bull? Couldn't he just go on with his life and forget
the blasted rodeo?

A stab of realization hit her, tearing through her
walls of defenses. She'd never been able to go on with
her life after Evan. When he died, she had, too, in a
way. She'd stopped living. She'd set out to prove to
herself that no one would ever be able to hurt her
again. But someone had. Kirk had.

No, she corrected herself. She'd hurt herself. She'd
rejected him. She'd pushed him away. She'd run away
from him. She hadn't understood his needs, his crazy,
selfish need.

Or was it?

Watching the door close behind her student, she thought of what Kirk had said about Bobby Joe. "Everybody needs someone to believe in them." His words had been proven true after Shannon had spoken with Bobby Joe's mother. Mrs. Dooley and Kirk had probably helped change Mr. Dooley's attitude.

Maybe that's what Kirk needed. Maybe this crazy idea of facing his fears was an effort to believe in himself again. Maybe all he really needed was someone to believe in him, like his grandfather and Trey had. Maybe Kirk needed her to believe.

Guilt gnawed at her when she realized she'd denied him that. She'd turned her back on him, withdrawn her trust, her faith. Her heart skidded to a halt, then thumped again at a frantic pace. What if his confidence still wavered like it had when he'd first started speech? What if he didn't believe?

She remembered Kirk explaining that a bull rider's confidence was as essential as good equipment. If a cowboy lacked confidence, he wouldn't last a second on one of those bulls.

Twisting her hands in her lap, she pictured Kirk, silent but determined, climbing on the back of the evil black bull. Her vision blurred with hot tears, shifting to the scene of Smiling Sam's death.

What if Kirk died? Could she live with herself? Could she live without him?

She'd tried for the past month not to miss him, but she felt as if one of her vital organs had been stolen. She needed him like she needed air to breathe. She wanted him with an insatiable hunger. She loved him.

Kirk's words came back to her, milling around in her brain and filling her with hope. "When it's all said and done, it'll be worth everything if I've made an impact, if I've touched someone in a p-p-profound way."

He had made a difference. With Bobby Joe. With the Dooleys. With her. She felt stronger for having known him.

But in the end she'd reverted back to her old fears, leaned on them for protection. She'd revisited her past, examined herself and realized new insights. Evan had seized each moment, not for reaffirmation of life, but as a challenge to death. Kirk, on the other hand, reached out and grabbed each opportunity. Because tomorrow *might* not come, through no fault of his own. He lived each moment as his last, pushing himself through the hard times and enjoying the good. Kirk took advantage of what life offered, not wasting a second of the precious time he'd been afforded.

And she knew she'd wasted so much of her own life. She'd closed herself off from others to protect her heart, when in reality she'd only hurt herself, deprived herself of love.

Kirk's past words branded her heart with his honesty. "It's what I do with the hours, days and years before that count, not how or when I die. I want to make each moment worth something."

What if he was her last chance at love? Would she condemn him...herself to a fruitless life? A wasted moment, she thought, made a wasted opportunity. She wouldn't let Kirk get away. Somehow she knew that

even if she only had him for a moment, a breath of
time, it would be worth it.

But first she'd have to drum up the courage and face
her fear. Just as Kirk had encouraged her to do. He
would help her. And maybe she would help him by
believing in him. Before it was too late.

Chapter Ten

He was hot. Hotter than he could ever remember. Sweat dampened his hair, rolled down the side of his face and coated the back of his shirt. His skin prickled from the heat. The roughness of his shirt and the tension electrified his nerves. Kirk ran his fingers through his sticky hair then settled his Stetson low over his brow. With his jaw clenched tight, he squinted against the arena lights and stared at Zorro.

Inside, he felt cold, stone-cold with dread.

The bull, black as the road that leads to hell, pawed the red dirt and snorted his challenge. His horns knocked against the metal railing, sounding warning bells in Kirk's head.

He knew exactly how the wicked horns felt forking him between the ribs. He knew the weight behind each kick, the force of those hooves plowing down on him. And he knew the result. The raw, aching result of his past year and Sam's death.

The pain, the hot, shooting pain, that had ripped through him like a hungry lion, biting into him with a vengeance, reminded him of what he wanted most to forget. But couldn't. Now, he had a new image, one that brought the bone-chilling fear home again, one of a friend being trampled by blood-caked hooves.

It was a possibility that Kirk faced again…willingly.

Touching the scar at his temple, he remembered with a clarity as real and jagged as this lingering reminder what other bruises, cuts and wounds he'd suffered. Although his leg seemed healed, his knee still caught when it rained or turned cold, like a needle jabbing him in the kneecap.

But today, with the June sun tipping over the horizon in a bronze glow, he felt ready. His mind seemed clear, focused, determined. His body felt primed, sharp, solid.

This bull, in a matter of eight seconds, would learn who had the staying power, who was stronger, braver, tougher. And Kirk would prove that to himself, too. He needed to face his own fear, a murky darkness that still resided deep down inside of him. He had to do this…for himself. Then he could walk away, once again proud, this time maybe whole, this time toward a future, free of his past.

His muscles tensed as he paced back and forth in front of the chute. Over and over in his mind he went through the motions and pictured how he would react, how he'd counter each of Zorro's moves. He had to be ready, he had to be on guard, prepared for anything.

"Kirk?" Trey's voice penetrated his deep concentration.

He turned toward his brother, whose face looked pensive and tight. He nodded once, an acknowledgement, but he couldn't think of anything to say. His mind remained occupied with his upcoming ride, and his gaze veered toward Zorro, watching, analyzing, challenging him with a hard stare.

"You ready?" Trey asked, stepping up beside him.

"Yep."

"Good." Trey dug the toe of his boot into the dirt. "That's good."

Kirk glanced at him, the strong profile that resembled his own. His brother's usually smiling lips seemed drawn into a thin, straight line. For a moment Kirk forgot his own troubles, forgot his need to ride, forgot the loneliness he felt without Shannon. He saw concern etched clearly in the lines around his brother's mouth and in the deep shadows surrounding his eyes. A worry that spoke volumes and brought back the accident with full force.

Not until Sam's death had Kirk really understood what his own brother had experienced when he'd wrecked. And now he faced the guilt of forcing his brother through another dark portal. Kirk couldn't promise where it might lead.

He'd been around rodeo long enough to know fate had a grim sense of humor. Sometimes plain old luck

helped a cowboy survive, sometimes guts and damn
good technique, and sometimes nothing... not even
the best... could outsmart, outmaneuver or slip
through death's lasso. It happened. He didn't like it,
but it was a fact. Something he'd accepted.

A quick image of Sam's funeral came to mind. A
blanket of white carnations had covered the casket. As
pallbearers, he and Trey had placed their bouton-
nieres on the grave site. The hardest moment came
when he'd paid his respects to Geena, looked into her
pale, drawn face, at her tear-swollen eyes, then held
her. He'd felt Sam's baby move restlessly in the womb.
His heart had stopped, his throat ached, his eyes
burned with unshed tears. Tears that he couldn't release. Tears that would acknowledge the sorrow and
exaggerate his fear.

The loss of a loved one wasn't something he wished
on anyone. Not his brother. And certainly not Shannon.

Maybe it was for the best that they'd gone their
separate ways. Maybe she couldn't handle her fear.
Had he been cruel to challenge her to do just that?

Kirk clapped Trey's shoulder in a reassuring manner, understanding the twisting anxiety that he, too,
felt. "This is my last ride."

"I know." Trey kept his eyes trained on Zorro.

"No matter what. Win, lose or d-d-draw."

"I know." Trey's voice sounded stiff, not his usual,
casual self. "I'll be here waitin'."

"I figured."

Trey looked at him then, his blue eyes piercing. "You just watch your backside."

"Always." Kirk gave a stiff grin. He didn't want his brother to suffer because of him, but he didn't know a way to dodge hurting him. Still, he appreciated his brother's support. He needed that now more than anything. Since he'd lost Shannon, he needed someone to believe in him. "Th-th-thanks."

Trey returned the smile. "Ride tough."

Kirk nodded, his confidence growing. "You got it."

The tangy scent of barbecue nipped at Shannon's senses, reminding her she hadn't eaten. Her stomach knotted, snarling its displeasure at even the thought of food. Her nerves tightened their hold as she twisted her hands together. Her gaze darted from the ticket booths to the crowded stands to the chutes along one end of the arena.

She hesitated only a fleeting second, her mind doubting, her heart overruling, before she stepped forward. Her pace quickened as she headed for her destination—Kirk.

The odors of animal sweat and waste devoured the smells of popcorn, sweet carbonated drinks and cotton candy. The Friday night crowd grew thicker around her, pressing in upon her like her fear.

Cowboy hats bobbed and weaved as heads bent or tilted back with a laugh. Boots shuffled, scooted and slid on the sawdust-covered concrete. Almost as if the tobacco-spitting cowboys and jeaned cowgirls contrived against her, they blocked her path, trying to keep her away from the man she loved.

Frustration burned through her. She weaved around the concession lines, apologized for stepping between people and swerved around a toddler who bobbled a foot-long hotdog in his short, stubby hands. Her footsteps slowed behind a lazy, meandering group. Their voices rose with laughter, and she grew annoyed. She sidestepped the short, rounded man whose belly hung over his belt buckle, her shoulder brushing his.

"Excuse me," she said hastily, moving on at a faster gait without a backward glance.

That afternoon she'd been delayed at school. The principal had stopped her in the parking lot to discuss the next faculty meeting. She'd rushed home to change into jeans and boots. But now she hoped that hadn't been a wasted effort. Already the rodeo had begun: the calf ropers had finished, and the bronc riders started. She had to find Kirk before the bull riding event.

She had to tell him before he rode . . . before it was too late.

Her gaze searched each group of cowboys, her eyes darting from tobacco-filled mouths to hard, glinting eyes. But she didn't see Kirk anywhere.

Somehow she knew he wouldn't be socializing or wandering about to ease his nerves. She knew he'd be standing beside Zorro's chute, watching and waiting and worrying.

And she wanted to be there with him, offer her support, tell him she believed.

Her boot heels clomped against the concrete steps that led down to the long walkway where the livestock were kept. She passed stalls with hay-munching horses and pens with bawling calves. A bustle of activity swarmed around her. Cowboys warmed up, stretching their muscles and jumping in place. Cooing softly, a barrel racer unsaddled her horse. The announcer's voice rumbled in the background as the next bronc rider sprang out of an open gate. The cheers of the crowd echoed around her.

Then she saw *him*.

With his head bent, his hat shading his face, he wrapped his rope around his hand over and over, drawing it tight then releasing it. Behind him, Zorro stared through the metal rails of his chute. Kirk repeated the same movements again. She noted the swiftness of his hands and width of his shoulders, his muscles and tendons bunching beneath his starched shirt. Tension lined his face, making the scar along his temple stand out like a stark, jagged line against his tanned face. Dark shadows accented his lowered eyes. His cheeks looked hollow, bracketing his mouth with deep lines.

Her heart jolted, and love surged within her. She wondered what went on in his head at a moment like this before he put it all on the line. Was he nervous? Afraid? Calm? She couldn't imagine anyone about to ride a ton of steel being cool and composed. Her hands shook. Her insides twisted. Her shoulders tensed. All for him.

She waited in the middle of the walkway, unable to move forward, refusing to turn away. Cowboys walked around her, a few glancing back. She waited for Kirk to see her. She waited for a sign of his acceptance. What that sign would be, she didn't know.

When he did look up, his hands froze, his eyes opened wide, and his gaze pierced a burning hole through her heart.

In that instant she wondered if she'd made a mistake. She'd heard Trey and Kirk talk about the importance of keeping their focus before a ride. Had she shattered his concentration? And threatened his life?

His gaze skimmed over her body, like a caress, bold and daring. She doubted herself for a moment. What if he spurned her? What if he told her he didn't need her? What if she never said anything at all, just turned and ran?

She couldn't walk away and never look back. She had to know he made it through this ride, even if he never wanted to see her again. If she left him, she'd never know what might have been. The unanswered question would haunt her forever. If she lost this chance, then what other chances might she also lose? She knew, beyond any doubts, that Kirk was worth risking her heart.

More than that, she knew this was something she had to do. After he'd worked so hard to restore his faith in himself, she couldn't yank away her support, leaving him stranded to face Zorro alone. That she couldn't handle. Even though the thought of watching him ride the bull turned her stomach inside out, and the possibility of him getting hurt made her heart pound in her chest, she had to tell him she believed in him.

She had to tell him she loved him.

Staring at him across the long section of hay-strewn walkway, with the musty straw scenting the air, she waited for that sign. But Kirk seemed tense, anxious, expectant. She realized that he had no idea what she wanted. When she focused on him, she took her first step forward, unwilling to look back, unwilling to let this moment pass.

She walked straight for him. Her knees wobbled like wet noodles. When she saw the glint in his gray eyes, she knew. His deep longing seared her. His intense gaze told her, even from a distance, that he needed her. It was the sign she'd wanted, hoped for, but only imagined.

Her hands twisting together, she stopped in front of him. Deafening silence became a barrier between them. Finally his mouth relaxed, curving into a half smile. She sighed, and her pulse raced. At least she knew he wouldn't send her away. He still wanted her. As much as she wanted him.

"Hello, Shannon," Trey said, walking up. He hooked his arm around her shoulders and gave her a brief, friendly hug.

Shannon couldn't look away from Kirk, and his eyes remained steady on her. The anticipation undulated between them like shock waves.

Trey clapped Kirk's shoulder. "It's about time."

Kirk nodded, looked back at the bull in the chute, then toward Shannon again. His eyes sparked, shining like metal. "W-w-will you wait?" He coughed, clearing his raspy voice. "I mean until I f-f-finish?"

She nodded. In his stutter, she sensed his underlying fear. Her eyes misted.

"We can talk then." He stepped backward, his wrist flicking the rope nervously. "I'm g-g-glad you came."

Before she could speak, he turned away, his spurs jingling. His broad shoulders stiffened. He readjusted his hat and hiked up his jeans. He paused there, looking at Zorro.

She wondered if this was his practiced prelude that he performed before every ride. Or if he was floundering with indecision. He stood before the chute for a long, drawn-out moment. Trey sat on the railing, waiting, and called to him once more. Then Kirk glanced over his shoulder at Shannon.

Her heart cracked in two. She wanted to help him. But she didn't know how. He fought a demon all his own, one she couldn't see or understand. But it was there all the same, igniting his soul, hurling him toward this beast.

Without thinking, she reached out and placed a hand on his arm. She felt his muscles jump, then the burning heat of his smoldering gaze. Her throat ached with the words she longed to say.

"I love you," she blurted out. "No matter what."

He blinked. Then he took a step toward her. His hands embraced her waist. His fingers felt warm and insistent, pulling her toward him. He tilted his head and placed a soft kiss on her lips. She melted against him, her lips parting with a sigh.

His arms tightened, his kiss became hard, intense, urgent. She raised up on her tiptoes and kissed him back. His mouth opened, their tongues met. She breathed in his scent, his taste. His arms held her against his solid chest, pressing her to him, molding her against him.

That was where she wanted to be forever... in his arms... secure in his love. *Please, God,* she prayed silently, *protect this man.*

Her fears magnified in her mind. What if this was the last time she saw him, held him, kissed him? What if Zorro hurt him? What if...?

She clung to his shoulders, desperate to hold on to him until the last possible second, unwilling to let him go, selfish in wanting to keep him safe with her.

His hands grazed her sides, his thumbs brushing the gentle slope of her breasts. A sweet yearning threaded through her. She felt his heart beating against her breast. Her heart answered with its own throbbing pulse. He fit her body to his until she felt every curve and nuance, his hard chest, belt buckle and jean-clad thighs. Desire ignited inside her, setting her body aflame.

She couldn't let him go... she wouldn't...

Suddenly she pushed against his chest. Afraid for him. Afraid for herself. If she held him a moment longer, she'd never release him. And he'd resent her interference.

He had to do this. He had to ride Zorro. For himself. It had nothing to do with her. And she didn't want to distract him, make him lose his focus.

Beneath the brim of his hat, he stared down at her, his eyes dark with desire. "I love you."

Her heart swelled, and tears brimmed her eyes, blurring her vision. She gave him a trembling smile and knew she'd done the right thing in coming tonight. Now she had to push him away and let him go. But she struggled within herself to find the strength to do that.

His hands squeezed her waist. The intensity of his feelings transmitted to her. His eyes locked on to hers with a hard, promising look. "I'll be back. I promise."

"I know you can do this. I . . . I came to tell you that." She gripped his hand, anxious to tell him all she'd come to say, yet frantic to release him before she couldn't.

The chute rattled as Zorro bucked. His blunted horns raked along the rails, sending shivers down Shannon's spine.

Kirk tilted his head toward Zorro. "I've got to go. . . ."

She nodded but held him in place with her steady gaze.

Before she could move away, he hugged her close. His embrace told her what words could not. Her fingers skimmed over his shoulders, memorizing each angle and outline from his collarbone down to his wrist. She inhaled his rugged male scent of sun, sweat and spicy cologne. She studied his dark, curling chest hair in the opening of his shirt and pressed her cheek against his warm neck.

"...Kirk Mann, folks..." The announcer's voice broke into her thoughts. "He's back again, ready to ride the most dangerous bull we got. And if any cowboy has the guts to ride this Brahma, Kirk does. This cowboy's tough as nails and feisty as a bullwhip."

"Kirk," Trey said, "let's go. You're up."

Her body stiffened, and she felt Kirk's shoulders sag briefly before he squared them. He held her close for a long moment, his breath hot against her ear. She ran her hands down his back, feeling the damp, sweat-soaked shirt. Her fingers curled into the hair at the base of his neck, trying to soothe his nerves.

"I believe," she whispered. "I believe in you."

His arms tightened, squeezing the breath out of her. She didn't care. She knew then that he needed her, needed her to help him face his fear. She found her own strength in that, knowing he loved her, wanted her, needed her.

Forcing herself to back out of his arms, she swallowed her fear and managed a watery smile. If he could be courageous and face his fear, then she could be brave and face hers. For him. This time she stepped away, giving him the freedom to do what he had to do, and blinking back the tears that threatened. "I'll be waiting."

His thoughts jumbled together, like a tiller churning the ground for planting. Tiny seeds of doubt landed in his mind, watered by his love for Shannon.

He shook his head, trying to focus, trying to concentrate on his ride. With his gloved hand, he grabbed the top rail and hauled himself up. He hitched his hip over the edge and stared down at Zorro. He watched the massive shoulder muscles flex. With one backward glance, he gave Shannon a reassuring smile.

God, he was glad she'd come. Hope soared within him, and possibilities loomed before him. She believed. She believed. And now he, too, believed.

He believed he could do anything—ride Zorro, lasso the moon, love Shannon forever. He wanted to give her everything; his heart wasn't enough. He wanted to place a glittering diamond on her finger, build her a house and give her children.

His confidence grew like stalks of corn beneath the summer sun, abundant and strong. His gaze flicked back to Zorro. He knew without a doubt he could do this. He felt it in his gut.

After mounting the bull, he wrapped his hand tight and settled himself high over the bulging shoulders. He wouldn't let himself get knocked back in the danger zone, wouldn't let himself get bucked off, wouldn't let anything happen to him. He had something to tell Shannon afterward, and nothing would jeopardize his future with her.

Feeling the hard-muscled flesh beneath him, he focused. He thought of Zorro. He concentrated on responding to each movement, ready to counter with his own. The bull bucked and slammed Kirk into the chute. The metal hinges rattled. The weathered floorboard groaned. Zorro leaned against that side, pinning Kirk against the rails, jamming his knee into the hard iron pole.

He grimaced, righted himself and spurred the Brahma in the flanks. The bull lurched sideways, his hooves scraping across the wood floor, and freed Kirk's leg.

With a sigh he looked up at Trey and grinned. "O-k-k-kay."

"This is gonna be fun," Trey said and clasped Kirk's shoulder in support.

This is it, he thought. This was what he'd worked for, what he needed to do. He was ready to finish this matter, get it behind him and move on.

"This here Brahma's a bounty bull, folks," the announcer said, his voice full of excitement. "That means he's worth about twelve thousand dollars if this cowboy can stay on him for eight seconds. Doesn't have to be flashy. He can hustle and scramble all he wants or make it purty as a picture. Don't matter. He's just gotta give this bull one heck of a ride."

The announcer paused. The crowd held their collective breaths. A stillness descended upon Kirk in the seconds before the gate clanged open. Trey waited for Kirk's signal.

Kirk heard only the rush of his blood racing through his veins, a pounding in his temples, his breath coming in short gasps through gritted teeth. He rocked back and forth on the bull, finding the perfect spot. His legs clenched the sides of the Brahma tight. With his free hand he touched the brim of his Stetson, ready to nod to Trey.

A soft noise broke his concentration, a muffled crying sound. He glanced over his shoulder and saw tears brimming in Shannon's eyes. One slipped down her porcelain cheek and nestled in the corner of her lips. Her forced smile wavered, her mouth glistening, quivering with faltering courage. His heart broke into shards of longing, cracking open his pride.

"You ready?" Trey asked. "Kirk? Hey! Get your head on straight."

He flinched, then realized, staring at Shannon's tear-filled hazel eyes, that this ride was meaningless. He had all he ever needed—Shannon.

"Kirk?" Trey called.

Kirk couldn't focus on his brother. From a distance he heard the encouragement of the crowd. Their enthusiasm for him to lay it all on the line echoed off the stands. He felt Zorro shift restlessly beneath him, eager to storm out of the chute.

He decided then that it wasn't worth the risk of crippling himself or losing his life. It wasn't worth seeing Shannon torn apart.

With his last two rides, he'd proven that he could return to the rodeo circuit, ride bulls without fear again. What else did he have to prove? Maybe she'd been right. Where would it end? What would ever be enough?

He shook his head, grabbed the rails and lifted himself off Zorro's back.

"What is it?" Trey asked, confusion lining his words. "What's wrong?"

Kirk ignored his brother and walked straight for Shannon.

The announcer's voice broke the quiet, "I don't know, folks, but it looks like this ride ain't gonna happen tonight. Next up is..."

"What are you doing?" Bewilderment darkened Shannon's eyes to almost green. Shaking her head, she backed away. "No." Her voice warbled with uncertainty. "Go back. Finish this." She sniffed, trying to control her tears.

Regretful that he'd brought her this much grief, he brushed a tear off her cheek with his thumb. He cupped her chin, caressing her jawline, feeling her softness and vulnerability. "I don't have to anymore."

"Why?" Her voice cracked.

He wrapped her in his arms, cradling her against his chest. "It's over. It's all over. I don't need this. I only need you."

"You aren't going to ride?" She stared at him as if in shock.

"No."

She embraced him, squeezing him as if to confirm he was there, in her arms. Her shoulders shook with silent sobs. He smoothed his hand down her back. She trembled against him and snuffled against his collar.

"I was wrong," she said, "so wrong. You're nothing like Evan. You proved that all along. I just couldn't see that. Not until now. Can you forgive me?"

"There's nothing to forgive." He brushed a kiss against her hair. He held her, smelled the light floral scent clinging to her hair, enjoyed her softness leaning into his hardness. Her fingers curled into the front of his shirt. He waited until her tears subsided.

Then he lifted her face to his. He stared into her wide, expressive eyes, loving the rich autumn colors hidden in their depths. This is right where he always wanted to be, holding her, loving her, needing her. Love blossomed within him, giving him the courage to speak his mind, his heart.

He thought of how much he loved her and of their future together. A future where they could take chances together, risks that were worth taking. He smiled at the woman he loved. "Shannon, will you marry me?"

She flung her arms around his neck and pulled him closer. In a rush of breath against his lips, she said, "Yes, Kirk. Oh, yes."

He stared down at her. His chest swelling with a love so intense, his throat closed and no more words would come. Instead of telling her, he'd have to show her in his own quiet way, for the rest of their lives, how much he loved her.

*   *   *   *   *

Shannon's love lassoed Kirk Mann—can a widow with a baby brand Trey with love and matrimony?
Find out in CHRISTMAS IN JULY by Leanna Wilson. It's coming in December from Silhouette Romance!

The exciting new cross-line continuity series about love, marriage—and Daddy's unexpected need for a baby carriage!

🥕🥕🥕🥕🥕🥕🥕🥕

You loved

THE BABY NOTION by Dixie Browning (Desire #1011 7/96)
and
BABY IN A BASKET by Helen R. Myers
(Romance #1169 8/96)

Now the series continues with...

MARRIED...WITH TWINS! by Jennifer Mikels
(Special Edition #1054 9/96)

The soon-to-be separated Kincaids just found out they're about to be parents. Will their newfound family grant them a second chance at marriage?

Don't miss the next books in this wonderful series:

HOW TO HOOK A HUSBAND (AND A BABY)
by Carolyn Zane (Yours Truly #29 10/96)

DISCOVERED: DADDY
by Marilyn Pappano (Intimate Moments #746 11/96)

DADDY KNOWS LAST continues each month...
only from *Silhouette*®

MILLION DOLLAR SWEEPSTAKES
AND EXTRA BONUS PRIZE DRAWING

No purchase necessary. To enter the sweepstakes, follow the directions published and complete and mail your Official Entry Form. If your Official Entry Form is missing, or you wish to obtain an additional one (limit: one Official Entry Form per request, one request per outer mailing envelope) send a separate, stamped, self-addressed #10 envelope (4 1/8" x 9 1/2") via first class mail to: Million Dollar Sweepstakes and Extra Bonus Prize Drawing Entry Form, P.O. Box 1867, Buffalo, NY 14269-1867. Request must be received no later than January 15, 1998. For eligibility into the sweepstakes, entries must be received no later than March 31, 1998. No liability is assumed for printing errors, lost, late, non-delivered or misdirected entries. Odds of winning are determined by the number of eligible entries distributed and received.

Sweepstakes open to residents of the U.S. (except Puerto Rico), Canada and Europe who are 18 years of age or older. All applicable laws and regulations apply. Sweepstakes offer void wherever prohibited by law. Values of all prizes are in U.S. currency. This sweepstakes is presented by Torstar Corp., its subsidiaries and affiliates, in conjunction with book, merchandise and/or product offerings. For a copy of the Official Rules governing this sweepstakes, send a self-addressed, stamped envelope (WA residents need not affix return postage) to: MILLION DOLLAR SWEEP-STAKES AND EXTRA BONUS PRIZE DRAWING Rules, P.O. Box 4470, Blair, NE 68009-4470, USA.

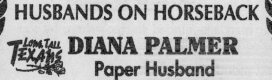

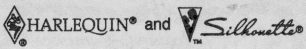

HARLEQUIN® and **Silhouette®**

are proud to present...

HERE COME THE GROOMS™

Four marriage-minded stories written by top
Harlequin and Silhouette authors!

Next month, you'll find:

Married?!	by Annette Broadrick
Designs on Love	by Gina Wilkins
It Happened One Night	by Marie Ferrarella
Lazarus Rising	by Anne Stuart

ADDED BONUS! In every edition of
Here Come the Grooms you'll find $5.00 worth
of coupons good for Harlequin and Silhouette
products.

On sale at your favorite Harlequin and Silhouette
retail outlet.

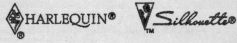

HARLEQUIN® **Silhouette®**

HCTG996

As seen on TV!
Free Gift Offer

With a Free Gift proof-of-purchase from any Silhouette® book,
you can receive a beautiful cubic zirconia pendant.

This gorgeous marquise-shaped stone is a genuine cubic
zirconia—accented by an 18" gold tone necklace.

(Approximate retail value $19.95)

Send for yours today…
compliments of  *Silhouette*®

To receive your free gift, a cubic zirconia pendant, send us one original proof-of-purchase, photocopies not accepted, from the back of any Silhouette Romance™, Silhouette Desire®, Silhouette Special Edition®, Silhouette Intimate Moments® or Silhouette Yours Truly™ title available in August, September or October at your favorite retail outlet, together with the Free Gift Certificate, plus a check or money order for $1.65 u.s./$2.15 can. (do not send cash) to cover postage and handling, payable to Silhouette Free Gift Offer. We will send you the specified gift. Allow 6 to 8 weeks for delivery. Offer good until October 31, 1996 or while quantities last. Offer valid in the U.S. and Canada only.

Free Gift Certificate

Name: _____

Address: _____

City: _____ State/Province: _____ Zip/Postal Code: _____

Mail this certificate, one proof-of-purchase and a check or money order for postage and handling to: SILHOUETTE FREE GIFT OFFER 1996. In the U.S.: 3010 Walden Avenue, P.O. Box 9077, Buffalo NY 14269-9077. In Canada: P.O. Box 613, Fort Erie, Ontario L2Z 5X3.

FREE GIFT OFFER   084-KMD
ONE PROOF-OF-PURCHASE
To collect your fabulous FREE GIFT, a cubic zirconia pendant, you must include this original proof-of-purchase for each gift with the properly completed Free Gift Certificate.

084-KMD

Who can resist a Texan...or a Calloway?

This September, award-winning author
ANNETTE BROADRICK
returns to Texas, with a brand-new
story about the Calloways...

SONS
→OF←
TEXAS

Rogues and Ranchers

CLINT: The brave leader. Used to keeping secrets.

CADE: The Lone Star Stud. Used to having women
fail at his feet...

MATT: The family guardian. Used to handling
trouble...

They must discover the identity of the mystery
woman with Calloway eyes—and uncover a
conspiracy that threatens their family....

Look for **SONS OF TEXAS:** Rogues and Ranchers
in September 1996!

Only from Silhouette...where passion lives.

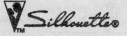

Silhouette®

SONSST

You're About to Become a

Privileged Woman

Reap the rewards of fabulous free gifts and
benefits with proofs-of-purchase from
Silhouette and Harlequin books

Pages & Privileges™

It's our way of thanking you for
buying our books at your
favorite retail stores.

PROOF OF PURCHASE

SR-PP171

Offer expires October 31, 1996

Harlequin and Silhouette—
the most privileged readers in the world!

For more information about Harlequin and
Silhouette's PAGES & PRIVILEGES program call the
Pages & Privileges Benefits Desk: 1-503-794-2499

Silhouette®

SR-PP171